Long ago and far away...

...there was a world filled with light and laughter and love. But quakes buried the land below the sea. Slowly the people adapted to their new world. But a civil war broke out, forcing the king of Pacifica to send his four children far away, each with a guardian and a piece of the royal seal.

Twenty-five years later, it was time for the siblings to be reunited—and reclaim what was lost. Saegar, the royal prince of Pacifica, had only vague memories of his homeland. Now he was ready to return, but first he must answer the call of a maiden in distress....

A Tale of the Sea

MORE THAN MEETS THE EYE by *Carla Cassidy*
IN DEEP WATERS by *Melissa McClone*
CAUGHT BY SURPRISE by *Sandra Paul*
FOR THE TAKING by *Lilian Darcy*

Dear Reader,

Summer is over and it's time to kick back into high gear. Just be sure to treat yourself with a luxuriant read or two (or, hey, all six) from Silhouette Romance. Remember—work hard, play harder!

Although October is officially Breast Cancer Awareness month, we'd like to invite you to start thinking about it now. In a wonderful, uplifting story, a rancher reluctantly agrees to model for a charity calendar to earn money for cancer research. At the back of that book, we've also included a guide for self-exams. Don't miss Cara Colter's must-read *9 Out of 10 Women Can't Be Wrong* (#1615).

Indulge yourself with megapopular author Karen Rose Smith and her CROWN AND GLORY series installment, *Searching for Her Prince* (#1612). A missing heir puts love on the line when he hides his identity from the woman assigned to track him down. The royal, brooding hero in Sandra Paul's stormy *Caught by Surprise* (#1614), the latest in the A TALE OF THE SEA adventure, also has secrets—and intends to make his beautiful captor pay...by making her his wife!

Jesse Colton is a special agent forced to play pretend boyfriend to uncover dangerous truths in the fourth of THE COLTONS: COMANCHE BLOOD spinoff, *The Raven's Assignment* (#1613), by bestselling author Kasey Michaels. And in Cathie Linz's MEN OF HONOR title, *Married to a Marine* (#1616), combat-hardened Justice Wilder had shut himself away from the world—until his ex-wife's younger sister comes knocking.... Finally, in Laurey Bright's tender and true *Life with Riley* (#1617), free-spirited Riley Morrisset may not be the perfect society wife, but she's exactly what her stiff-collared boss needs!

Happy reading—and please keep in touch.

Mary-Theresa Hussey

Mary-Theresa Hussey
Senior Editor

Please address questions and book requests to:
Silhouette Reader Service
U.S.: 3010 Walden Ave., P.O. Box 1325, Buffalo, NY 14269
Canadian: P.O. Box 609, Fort Erie, Ont. L2A 5X3

Caught by
Surprise

SANDRA PAUL

SILHOUETTE *Romance*®

Published by Silhouette Books

America's Publisher of Contemporary Romance

Special thanks and acknowledgment are given to Sandra Paul for her contribution to the A TALE OF THE SEA series.

Dedicated to all the wonderful and resilient women of New York, especially those at Silhouette. You guys are the best.

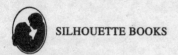 **SILHOUETTE BOOKS**

ISBN 0-373-19614-8

CAUGHT BY SURPRISE

Visit Silhouette at www.eHarlequin.com

Printed in U.S.A.

Books by Sandra Paul

Silhouette Romance

Last Chance for Marriage #883
The Reluctant Hero #1016
His Accidental Angel #1087
The Makeover Takeover #1559
Caught by Surprise #1614

Silhouette Yours Truly

Baby on the Way

Harlequin Duets

Head Over Heels
Baby Bonus?
Moonstruck

SANDRA PAUL

married her high school sweetheart and they live in Southern California with their three children, their dog and their cat.

She loves to travel, even if it's just several trips a month to her hometown bookstore. Bookstores are her favorite place to be.

Her first book with Silhouette Romance was the winner of RWA Golden Heart Award and a finalist for an RWA RITA® Award.

A TALE OF THE SEA

Family Tree

King Okeana (d.) m. Queen Wailele (d.)

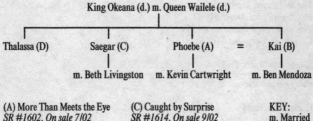

Thalassa (D) Saegar (C) Phoebe (A) = Kai (B)

m. Beth Livingston m. Kevin Cartwright m. Ben Mendoza

(A) More Than Meets the Eye
SR #1602, On sale 7/02

(B) In Deep Waters
SR #1608, On sale 8/02

(C) Caught by Surprise
SR #1614, On sale 9/02

(D) For the Taking
SR #1620, On sale 10/02

KEY:
m. Married
d. Deceased
= Twins

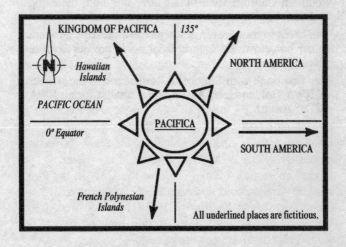

Prologue

They were hot on his tail.

Pushing aside his growing desperation, he concentrated on escape. His powerful arms sliced through the cold sea while his leanly muscled lower body enhanced each butterfly stroke with a graceful, curving thrust. Ignoring the burning in his lungs, he kept his head down, unwilling to waste the millisecond it would take to draw a breath.

He gained a yard. Then another. He was fast—very fast. But he'd be a fool to believe he could outrace a motorboat forever. Nor would the men chasing him give up. Their greedy excitement vibrated the air above him as clearly as the boat's motor vibrated the water.

He had to dive, quickly and deeply. Only in the dark, endless depths could he evade them. Another stroke, another slight gain. The rough, salty water flowed along his body like an icy caress. It was now or never. He soared higher to steepen his plunge—

And they struck. Fiery pain pierced his shoulder. He

jerked, managed to break loose from the jagged steel, but failed to escape the net that followed.

Fiercely he fought the tangling strands. If he'd had his knife, he could have cut himself free as he'd once done to escape a patch of tenacious seaweed in the soft surf near his home. But his knife lay on the sandy ocean floor, and the clingy web tightened with each desperate twist that he gave.

He would have kept struggling, courting death, if death would have helped his people. But it wouldn't. Dead or alive, his capture would prove their existence and send more greedy men out on the hunt.

So he stilled, conserving his energy as they hauled him to the surface. He almost welcomed the raw burn from the ropey twine scraping his skin; the sharp, pulsing fire from the wound in his shoulder. Pain would keep him alert. Anger would keep him focused.

He kept his expression blank as the fading sunlight glinted over his body, but inwardly he cursed the men staring at him with fearful fascination in their eyes. Even more, he cursed himself for the relentless curiosity that had driven him to gamble with his freedom.

But most of all, he cursed the pale-limbed female with the flowing brown hair who had lured him too close to danger. From the bow of her ship, she'd signaled for help using the ancient gestures of his people.

And he vowed revenge.

Chapter One

The combination lock on the hold door took forever to undo, and once inside, the slick railing of the spiraling staircase felt cold and clammy beneath Beth's palm. She should have changed out of her heels into canvas deck shoes, she realized belatedly as she slowly descended into the ship's hold. The metal steps were slippery. She certainly should have changed her evening dress for something more practical. The delicate blue silk would be ruined if sea water—or heaven forbid, fish bait or something equally disgusting—should happen to touch its gleaming folds.

Carefully holding her skirt away from the damp metal, Beth took another cautious step down—then gasped as the ship suddenly pitched. Clutching at the railing with both hands, she kept her balance. Barely. But when the ship rolled a second time her stomach went right along with it.

"Oh, darn, not again," she groaned, shutting her eyes. She hated it when a storm drew near, triggering her seasickness. In fact, she hated the sea entirely with its endless up and down, up and down motion and the scary mystery of its dark, cold depths. If it was up to her, she'd remain on dry land every second of her life, she decided, as the ship heaved once again.

But it wasn't up to her—not entirely. Because her father loved the sea and Carl T. Livingston was a certifiable genius who'd made enough from his biotechnological discoveries to indulge his every whim, including buying the huge, costly ship *The Searcher*. Unfortunately, his whims included putting a saltwater tank down in the hold of the vessel—a massive tank with a powerful pump, more than adequate to contain whatever creature his crew might capture for him to study.

Swallowing hard to force down her nausea, Beth opened her eyes and took another slow step downward. She wasn't anxious to discover what they'd caught this time. She always felt sorry for the sea animals the men scooped up for her father to examine. Dolphins, seals—once even a small octopus so confused by its confinement that it had huddled near the tank bottom, futilely grasping the small rock it had been clinging to when the men had prodded it into their net. The little octopod had refused to swim around; it had refused to eat. And before Beth could convince her father to release it, the baby octopus had died.

Pushing aside the memory, she slowly kept going, wrinkling her nose as the pungent odors of machine oil and brine rose up to greet her. She hoped this new creature didn't die. Especially since she'd been the one to cause its capture.

She hadn't meant to. She'd been standing on the bow of the ship the previous evening, fighting the urge to vomit, when her father's assistant had joined her.

She hadn't wanted company, and certainly not Ralph Lesborn's. Not that Ralph was unattractive. Tall and in his early thirties, Ralph's thick, reddish-blond hair was always neatly combed, and beneath his classically straight nose, a stylishly thin mustache outlined his full mouth.

Beth had been pleased for her dad when Ralph had agreed to come work aboard *The Searcher* a couple of months ago, but lately Ralph had developed the tendency to stand too close; it made her uneasy. And uneasiness was the last thing she wanted to feel when her stomach was already doing somersaults.

Sure enough, Ralph had crowded next to her by the rail. The sickly sweet smell of the cologne he favored caught in her throat, and the flattery he murmured in her ear made her feel sicker than the biggest heaving wave. Perhaps because he considered himself a gourmet, Ralph's compliments always seemed to involve food. She managed not to gag at the one about her eyes being as green as spinach—they were blue, for heaven's sake—but when he'd cooed something about her long hair being the same color as the bran muffins he ate each morning, she'd been sure she'd lose it all over his hand-made leather shoes.

She was rolling her eyes in revulsion when she'd glimpsed a golden tail fin flip up out in the water. Hoping to distract Ralph from her bran muffin hair, she'd pointed to the strange fish in the distance.

The ploy had worked. Ralph had stiffened—red mustache quivering, long eyes narrowing—looking remarkably like a cat who'd spotted a fish in a bowl. "No...I don't believe it. My God, it is!" he'd muttered almost beneath his breath. Then he'd hurried away to gather two of the crew, who'd quickly lowered the speedboat into the water and taken off.

Beth hadn't stayed to watch as they'd chased the poor thing down. Sending up a silent prayer for its escape, she'd slipped away to the stuffy sanctuary of her room.

But unfortunately, they had caught the creature. Her father had refused to tell her what it was when they'd dined together earlier, but his excitement had been almost palpable. Only by promising to go see it herself and report right back to him, had she managed to dissuade him from trying to leave his bed.

Yep, the hold gave her the creeps, but there wasn't much she wouldn't do for her father these days, Beth reflected, grimacing as her foot slipped again. *Precarious* was the word the doctors had used six months ago when discussing Carl's health after his latest heart attack. He seemed to fall victim to every virus going around, and just this week, had been laid up with the flu.

Not only was his physical health failing, but his mental health seemed to be deteriorating as well. Her heart ached as his once agile mind struggled to separate reality from illusion. She fought despair as he insisted on relentlessly searching the seas for the mythical beings that only existed in his confused brain.

She had long given up trying to make him abandon his hunt. All she wanted anymore was for him to be happy. So she wore evening gowns during their early dinners every day just to see a faint look of pleasure on his gaunt face. She tried to appreciate Ralph and his ridiculous, food-related compliments. And if her father wanted her to look at his mysterious fish and report back to him, then that's what she would do.

Finally reaching the last step, she paused to glance

over at the tank and the massive filter pump humming beside it. She'd hoped to check the fish out from the staircase. Since the tank was constructed of the same clear, indestructible acrylic as those used at public aquariums, she could usually see through it quite easily. But not this time.

The lighting wasn't the problem. The electric lamps scattered along the walls couldn't erase the shadows in the cavernous room, but a porthole cut high near the ceiling provided more than enough light to see. Even this late in the afternoon, the sunlight shone down through the thick, round window just like a spotlight, sparkling on the water below.

No, the real problem had been caused by the sea animal. It had churned the water—already disturbed by the pitching of the ship—into such a foaming whirlpool that only brief glimpses of its golden tail could be seen as it glided past.

"Darn it," she muttered, making a face. "I'll have to get closer."

Lifting her skirt higher, she made her way across the slimy floor, carefully stepping around the biggest wet patches. "What on earth is in there?" she wondered aloud as she neared the tank. She paused a couple yards away, trying to peer through the frothing water. Not a dolphin, she decided. Nor a seal, either.

It had to be some kind of shark.

She wasn't quite sure why she thought so. She'd certainly never heard of a golden shark. Yet, there was something about the way the creature moved, a lethal menace in its sensuous glide through the water, that reminded her irresistibly of those deadly sea predators.

A sudden thought made her pulse leap. Could it be a *mutant* shark, maybe? Now that would be a discovery—

maybe a big enough discovery to restore her father's reputation.

Budding hope replaced her reluctance. Moving right up to the side of the tank, she strained to see through the thick acrylic. A low, wooden platform hovered only a few feet over the surface of the water, but no way was she climbing up on that. With her luck, she'd fall in and the big fish would chomp her to bits.

The creature whipped by again. Her skin prickled, but she ignored her body's instinctive reaction to the danger the shark represented, refusing to back away. It couldn't get her here, after all—it was trapped in the tank. Besides, maybe it wasn't a shark but just a large tuna or an oversize sea bass. Anxious to find out, she wiped off the condensation that had built on the walls with her palm, creating a small clear circle. Again the creature swept past. Again, all she caught was a blur of movement. "Darn! What is it?"

Determined not to miss it again, she flattened her nose against the tank—and froze.

"Good heavens!" A man was in there with the creature! Floating right before her eyes, less than two feet away!

His dark hair billowed out gently in the water creating an incongruously soft frame for a profile that wasn't soft at all. High cheekbones, a bony jaw, an imperious high-bridged nose—the dominant cast of his features gave him the look of a Roman warrior. But his golden, sun-tanned skin, his broad, muscular shoulders—those were pure California surfer.

She gestured frantically to get his attention. "What are you doing? Are you crazy?" she demanded, her throat tight with alarm. "There's a giant, scary—*something*—in there! You have to get out!"

She knocked on the tank and he turned his head. Beth sucked in a breath as his gaze locked with hers. His eyes… Never before had she seen such mesmerizing eyes. They were blue. Not an indeterminate blue like her own, but rather a true midnight. So dark as to appear almost black. So fathomless, she could feel the fine hairs prickle on the back of her neck as he looked deep into her soul.

For endless seconds they stared at each other through the slowly surging water. Then she wrenched her gaze away, swallowing to ease her dry throat.

He simply continued to watch her, not appearing concerned at all. Was he some kind of daredevil perhaps? Or a Greenpeace activist? Who was he? Not that it mattered, she thought in rising panic. Whoever he was, he had to get out of that tank before the mutant shark got him!

Her growing alarm must have been reflected on her face, because for the barest second, his enigmatic expression changed. Was it disdain—contempt?—that flashed across his face? Beth couldn't be sure…and she forgot the question as he slowly swept his hand downward.

Instinctively, she followed the movement. Her gaze drifted down past his broad shoulders to his muscular chest, lingered for a second on the silver medallion lying against his golden skin, then dropped even lower to his washboard stomach and lean masculine hips. They were encased in some kind of odd, glittery suit, she realized, as he shifted slightly. A scaled suit. A golden scaled suit that covered his legs, his ankles, even his feet and ended in a…

Tail?

The mutant's tail—golden and glittering. But not a

mutant shark's as she'd first surmised, but rather a mutant man's. A mythical man described in ancient legends, the kind of being her father had been hunting for years. To be precise, a creature who was half fish, half human.

A *merman.*

Chapter Two

No— Yes! It couldn't be...but it was! The evidence was floating right before her eyes. Beth felt dazed, unable to look away from that unbelievable tail. Logic and disbelief warred in her brain, freezing her in place. She couldn't breathe. Couldn't move.

But he could. Her wide gaze grew even wider as the man—the fish—the *whatever* he was—suddenly shot to the surface of the tank. He hovered there a moment looking down at her...then turned and slapped his tail, sending a large wave lapping over the side.

Drenching Beth completely.

"Omigosh!" The shock of the icy water broke her paralysis. She turned to run, almost tripping over the sodden skirt of her gown as she stumbled back toward the staircase. She lost one shoe, then the other. She didn't care. Not about that or how slimy the floor felt. Or the way the cold metal steps seemed to burn her bare feet as she scampered up them. Sheer blind panic—triggered by a primitive fear of the unknown—had her in its grip. All she cared about was getting away from that fish-man. Out of the gloom to safety.

She'd almost reached the top of the staircase when something grabbed her dress, yanking her to a halt. Him? Free of the tank? Her heart jumped into her throat. Clinging to the rail for support, she glanced behind her.

Her skirt had snagged on a rusty screw.

With a gasp of relief, she tore free. She fell, bruising her knee, but immediately scrambled up and kept going, running out the door, slamming it behind her. She took two steps—then paused.

The lock. She'd promised her father she'd relock the door.

Whirling around, she spun the combination until it clicked to a halt, then hurried off to her father's stateroom. She tried to walk, but her steps kept quickening until at last—finally!—she burst through his door.

Carl Livingston stared at her across an expanse of plush maroon carpet. Alarm flashed across his gaunt face, and he struggled to sit up in his bed. "Elizabeth! My goodness, child, you're all wet!"

Then he saw her expression. He stilled, leaning on his elbow with his eyes fixed on hers. "So it's true—Ralph wasn't mistaken." His voice sounded oddly hushed. "We caught a mermaid."

Beth shivered. "Actually," she said, wrapping her arms around her waist to still her shaking, "you caught a *mermale*."

Light flared in Carl's sunken eyes. For a few precious seconds wonder eased the lines of suffering around his mouth and brow. "I knew they were out there," he declared almost dreamily, his thin cheeks flushing with rare color. "I first sighted one in these very waters—a beautiful female with long, dark hair floating on the waves.

Nearly twenty years ago it was, only a few months after your mother died..." His voice trailed off on the final sentence. A spasm of pain crossed his features and he fell back against the pillows, coughing.

Beth glanced around the room, and realized her father's nurse must have gone to the galley for her dinner break. "I'll go get Anne," she said, turning back toward the door.

Carl's voice stopped her. "No," he wheezed, still coughing sporadically, but shaking his head. "Stay here. We need to talk."

Beth leaned against the doorjamb. Pushing her wet hair back from her face with a trembling hand, she forced her own breathing to slow while she waited for her father's coughing spell to stop.

Carl's paroxysm finally eased. He rested for a few moments against the pillow, staring up at the mahogany-paneled ceiling. Then he turned his head to look at her again. The color in his face had faded, but his gaze still held the glittering sharpness it used to have whenever one of his theories had proven correct as he asked, "How did he look?"

Beth stared back at him unseeingly, images whirling in her mind. *A bronzed, muscular chest. Shimmering, golden scales.* "Incredible," she whispered. *Hard-edged features and a dark, fathomless gaze.* "Dangerous," she added with a shudder. "Dad, that merman is very, very angry."

She jumped as Ralph spoke from behind her. "Please, keep your voice down, Elizabeth," he admonished her. With a murmured apology, he brushed past her into the room, closing the door deliberately behind him. "We want to keep the merman's existence a secret for the time being."

She stared at him in astonishment. "A secret! The whole crew must know about him by now."

Ralph shook his head. "No, they don't. Even the captain has no idea what we've captured. Only you, your father, and the Delano brothers know what's actually in the tank. After we netted our find, I wrapped him up in canvas before we brought him back to the ship. Oh, the rest of the men probably know we've snared something of interest," he admitted, "but who among them would ever suspect the truth?"

"I knew that one day we'd find one," Carl declared with pride in his voice. "It was just a matter of time."

"And you were right, sir," Ralph agreed fervently. His pale eyes lit with excitement as he added, "Think of the coverage, the attention, this will garner when it hits the media. A live merman! We'll be famous!"

Nausea twisted in Beth's stomach. She didn't want to be famous. She just wanted that merman off the ship. Back in the sea where he belonged before he did something more dangerous than splashing her.

"But he hates being in that tank," she protested, glancing from Ralph to her father. "He threw water all over me!"

"An accident, I'm sure," Ralph told her. "If anything he's probably just playful. Apt to splash a bit if one gets too close…" His gaze swept over her, and disapproval thinned his full mouth. "As you apparently did."

Glancing down, Beth realized what a mess she was. Her gown was ruined; her bra showed clearly through the wet material. Crossing her arms protectively across her chest, she opened her mouth to argue, but Ralph cut her off with a wave of his stocky hand.

"You've had a shock," he said in a soothing tone that merely annoyed her. "Let me get you a towel.

You're dripping all over your father's carpet." Without waiting for her answer, he headed into the adjoining bathroom.

He's worried about the carpet? Beth thought in amazement. When there was a merman down in the hold?

"Listen to me," she insisted, watching him through the open door. "That merman is really upset."

"Nonsense, Elizabeth. You're the one who's upset." Ralph opened a cupboard and reached inside. "The merman doesn't have real emotions. Not like people do."

She stared at him in surprise. "You can't know that."

"Of course I can. I've been observing him most of the day," Ralph informed her as he came back into the room. "We've made numerous efforts to communicate, but the creature hasn't responded at all—not even on the most primitive level. He can't understand a thing."

"If anyone should know, Ralph should," her father reminded her. "His expertise is working with sea mammals."

"But he hasn't worked with mermen—no one has," Beth pointed out. "And I'm sure the merman understands something at least. Why, he's wearing some kind of medallion around his neck. Would a fish do that?"

Amusement caused Ralph's mustache to twitch. "Sometimes. I've trained dolphins to slide chains around their necks, after all. Perhaps he picked it up from the bottom of the ocean and slipped it on. Chimps put things around their necks, too. Even in the wild."

"But he's not a dolphin or a chimp! He's half-human—"

"Shush, you're getting all excited." Draping the towel around her, Ralph brought the ends together beneath her chin and looked down into her face. "Don't be deceived by appearances," he chided softly. "It's not a man, just a fish. With no more sensibility than a cichlid in a bowl."

His thick knuckles nudged her chin, encouraging her to meet his eyes. Aware of her father watching, Beth forced herself to do so. Ralph's pale eyes looked sincere, confident. Her worry eased a little…yet refused to disappear completely. The merman had looked so—so intense.

She stepped away, forcing Ralph to release his grip. Clutching the towel closer around her, she turned back to her father. "Even a fish can feel pain."

Carl smiled reassuringly at her. "Of course they can, my dear. But he's not in pain…or at least—" he hesitated, glancing at his assistant "—did you tend to that wound yet, Ralph?"

"No, not yet, sir."

"He's hurt?" Beth glanced at Ralph in concern. "Where? I didn't see anything."

"It's on his back. High up on his shoulder. Rather minor, in my opinion."

"How did it happen?"

Ralph shrugged, spreading his hands in puzzlement. "Who knows? Maybe he scraped himself on some coral. Or possibly got bitten by another fish. It's hard to say until I have a chance to examine the injury more closely."

He glanced over at her father as he added, "I'll have to contain him in a smaller crate in order to do that, sir. We'll get right on it tomorrow. I thought it would be best to give him a chance to settle down in the tank today. To acclimate himself to his new environment."

Carl nodded with approval. "Good idea."

"Yes, that is a good idea," Beth agreed. "If the

wound needs attention, then take care of it. And after that…'' Taking a deep breath, she resolutely met her father's eyes. ''Well, after that, I think you should let him go.''

''Let him go!'' Carl's incredulous tones cut off Ralph's exclamation of protest. He stared at his daughter in amazement. ''Elizabeth, do you realize what you're asking?''

She clasped her hands tightly together. ''I know this has been your lifelong quest—''

''Not just my quest—the quest of every man throughout history who's ever glimpsed the creatures,'' Carl said, his voice rising sharply. ''The Greeks—the Romans. Even Captain John Smith spied a mermaid in 1614 when he reached the coast of Maine. But I am the first—*the very first man in thousands of years*—to actually manage to capture one of the creatures.'' His thin chest heaved as he gasped for breath, but the intensity of his gaze didn't ease. ''And you want me to let him go?''

Beth stared back at him helplessly. ''Yes. It's amazing—wonderful—that you found him,'' she said, trying to calm him down. ''But we can't just kidnap him—''

''Kidnap!'' Ralph laughed heartily. Putting his arm around her shoulders, he gave her a squeeze. ''Elizabeth, Elizabeth. Your imagination is running wild. You can't kidnap a sea animal. We're simply holding him in the name of science.''

''Well, can't we simply videotape him?'' she asked with sudden inspiration. ''Take some pictures and release him?''

Ralph released her instead. ''You're being naive,'' he told her, with a hint of contempt. ''No one will believe a videotape. This is the kind of find that scientists will insist on seeing for themselves.''

Carl nodded somberly. "He's right, Elizabeth. No one knows that better than I do. In fact, Ralph has convinced me to keep our find a secret for a couple of weeks until the Fall Science Exposition opens in San Diego. We'll gain more validity by revealing the merman there, where the world's scientists can see for themselves that it isn't a hoax.''

"But, Dad…''

He waved her to silence, and lay quietly for a moment. Staring unseeingly ahead, he collected his thoughts, his thin, restless fingers plucking at the blue silk bedspread lying across his legs. Then he looked back at Beth. His mouth twisted as he slowly admitted, "It hurt, daughter, to have lifelong colleagues turn away from me the way they did when I announced my belief in the existence of mermaids. I don't know what I would have done if you hadn't believed in me, and I want your support now, too.''

Guilt—hot and heavy—flooded Beth's chest. The truth was, she hadn't believed in him. She loved him with all her heart—she worried about him constantly— but not since she was a little girl had she considered the notion that his claim might be valid.

Until today.

She stifled a sigh. Who was she to think she knew better than he did? She'd majored in sociology, not marine biology. Besides, she'd only seen the merman for a minute or so—met his eyes for barely seconds. Even if it had been anger in his gaze, that didn't make him human. Animals got angry, too. Maybe he didn't mind being in the tank as much as she thought. If Ralph—who'd worked with sea mammals for over a decade—was sure the merman had the sensibility of a fish, then who was she to say differently?

In fact, maybe it was even a *good* thing that they'd caught him, so Ralph could tend to the wound on his shoulder. Perhaps the merman would have died if they hadn't captured him.

She looked over at her father, lying there so pale and thin. So sick with his damaged heart. She thought of the years, the decades, he'd been on his search. All he'd given up to pursue it. If she hadn't had faith in him before, wouldn't now be a good time to start?

Her father met her gaze, entreaty and pride combined in his own. "Don't you understand, Bethie? This find will restore my reputation, my standing in the scientific community. You want that, don't you?"

Tears prickled behind her eyelids. Did he really need to ask? "Of course I do."

The tension eased from his body. With a sigh, he shut his eyes.

Weariness washed over Beth as well. Suddenly conscious of her wet clothes, she turned to leave. "I'd better go change."

She reached for the doorknob, and Ralph immediately stepped forward to open it for her. Perhaps he saw the trouble on her face, because he suggested, "Why don't you come and watch us work with the merman tomorrow, Elizabeth? It will give you a chance to learn a thing or two about the creatures."

"I don't think so," she said quietly as she slipped past. "I already know enough as it is."

Down in the hold, the merman circled the tank, flashes of rage still surging through him. The saltwater whipped along his skin, stung his open wound, but still he kept going. Ignoring the increasing pain in his torn shoulder, he let each powerful motion of his arms and tail flow fluidly into the next.

Such a deceitfully sweet face his captor had. Such false distress in her sea-colored eyes.

He churned the water harder—faster. Yet even its loud grumbling in his ears could not drown out the thoughts of the little female tumbling through his mind.

Her voice had been soft yet lilting, like water murmuring merrily over sea stones. She'd stared at him as if she knew him—yet feigned surprise at the sight of his tail.

He passed the place where she'd stood. Then passed it again. From the corner of his eye, he glimpsed a mark on the tank's clear wall. He faltered, destroying his rhythm. Jerking to a halt, he stared at the circle she'd made with her small hand, her image surfacing in his mind once again.

Slim arched brows. A delicate nose and winsome red mouth. Smooth skin that glowed like a pearl. She wore her thick brown hair long, like the females of his people. Streaked with the mellow gold of ancient doubloons, it cascaded down her back, the ends frothing in playful curls.

Glancing away with a silent curse, he surged upward, exploding out of the water in a violent burst of energy. Flinging back his hair, he stared measuringly at the low platform hanging over the water.

If he were but mer, like his sisters, escaping would be no problem. But he was meremer, one of the cursed ones. For him, there was no transforming back and forth from mer to human between land and sea.

He glanced at the high porthole then turned to study

the door at the top of the twisting staircase. A low growl rumbled in his throat.

Like a princess she had descended, wrinkling her nose, holding her skirt high. Stepping over the small puddles on the floor with dainty precision.

His eyes narrowed with grim satisfaction at the memory of how she had left, fleeing from this pit with water streaming down her hair and dress. A minor revenge, but he'd enjoyed the sweet taste of it nonetheless. It fed his hunger for more.

He began swimming again, relentlessly working his arm lest the wound in his shoulder should become tight and stiff. He was not worried that he might have startled her away for good. He'd seen the fear in her blue-green eyes…but he'd seen the curiosity, as well.

It was the same ill-fated curiosity that had drawn him to her when she'd stood on the bow of her ship.

His jaw tightened, his strokes grew faster. Aye, she would be back. Like the turning of the tide beneath the full moon, her return was inevitable.

And so was his escape.

Chapter Three

Yep, if anyone knew about mermaids she did, Beth reflected the next day as she sat in the shadows at the top of the staircase in the hold. Everything from the Disney classic to ancient texts of mermaid lore. In fact, due to her father's obsession, she'd probably be considered an expert on the subject.

As a child she'd listened for hours as—minute detail by detail—he'd recited the descriptions of the sea people documented by the Roman historian Pliny the Elder. Or reviewed aloud the eyewitness account given by the esteemed Bishop Pontoppidan of Norway, who vouched for a mermaid netted at Hordaland in Bergen Fjord.

She knew that a Greek named Alexander had been the first to describe a mermaid complete with a fish tail—reportedly a lovely creature who burst into tears when a curious crowd examined her, then dived back into the water, yelling unintelligible curses as she swam off. And as a teenager Beth had practically memorized the stories about the fifty beautiful daughters of Nereus, a god of the sea. Apparently, they rode the waves on the backs of dolphins, and had many fantastic adventures.

Yes, she'd heard them all—fables of sea sirens who saved ships or foretold the future or lured sailors to a watery grave. Stories of mermaids with green hair, or feathers, or scales they could remove when they wanted to live on land but had to wear when they returned to the water. She knew legends of potent mariners who'd married mermaids and went on to found dynasties of great navigators because, after all, who would know the sea better than the creatures who lived there?

How fiercely she'd longed as a little girl to actually see one of the lovely, mystical beings. And how she'd wished, even more desperately in recent years, for some proof that her father wasn't completely delusional.

Well, now she had it—both her wishes granted in the form of one restless bundle of male energy trapped in the tank below. Be careful what you wish for, she thought wryly.

She stifled a sigh. As she shifted to ease the numbness in her bottom caused by sitting so long on the metal step, her hand brushed a sticky patch on the railing by her side. Making a face at the machine oil on her fingers, she bent over to try to wipe it off on the metal step at her feet. She probably had it all over her jeans and red silk shirt, she thought in disgust. The light was so shadowy at the top of these stairs.

She'd lurked in the dimness for over two hours now, unnoticed by the men below. Which was exactly what she wanted. She didn't plan to interfere—or even make her presence known. She hadn't even intended to come watch. Her instincts kept telling her to get as far from the merman as she possibly could yet, at the same time, she hadn't been able to stay away.

A fearful curiosity was part of what drew her back, she admitted silently to herself. The same kind of feeling that caused people to slow down and gawk at the scene of a car accident. Or pick up the *National Enquirer* to read about the latest sighting of fanny-faced aliens landing in the Arizona desert.

But even more than any of that was the disquiet she still felt. An odd niggling uneasiness that just refused to disappear. Worry for the people around the merman; and a bit of worry for the merman himself.

Not that she'd seen any evidence to support either. As he'd said, all that Ralph and his two helpers did was watch the merman swim endlessly around the tank. Beth kept watching too, but like the previous day, she wasn't able to see much from the staircase. Just an occasional glimpse of a dark head, or flash of a golden tail fin, flipping up through the foaming water. But even those brief glimpses made her breath catch and her heartbeat quicken. Fish mentality or not, the merman was definitely a fascinating creature. She could hardly look away.

Ralph didn't take his eyes off him, either. Her father's assistant had changed from his dress shirt and slacks into a set of work clothes he kept in a small supply behind the stairs. Dressed all in black—shirt, pants and even shoes—he stood on the wooden platform built out over the tank. Hands behind his back, rocking on his heels every now and then, Ralph kept turning to keep the merman in sight. Like the ringmaster in a circus, Beth mused. The effect was heightened by the light shining down on him from the porthole above.

Unlike Ralph, the Delano brothers stood in the shadows, well back from the tank. They were watching the merman, too, Beth noticed, as she glanced their way.

She studied them, wondering what they thought of the creature they'd helped capture. She certainly couldn't tell much from their expressions. Ralph had once told her the men were twins, but beyond having the same olive-toned skin and dark hair, the brothers didn't look much alike.

Small and wiry, Little Dougie Delano's shrewd expression and quick movements—not to mention his long pointed nose and buck teeth—gave him an unfortunate resemblance to a rat. Standing next to his brother, Big Mike appeared as huge and stolid as a baby elephant. Legs spread, slowly swaying back and forth, he stared at the tank with his mouth agape, dull surprise briefly lighting his fleshy face every time the merman passed.

Around and around the merman kept swimming, without any noticeable decrease in the speed or power he'd displayed from the start. Fifteen more minutes slipped by. Thirty. Beth was just thinking that the merman would swim endlessly, when Ralph gave a shout.

"He's tiring, boys! Get ready to get to work."

Unconsciously, Beth stiffened, leaning forward. At first, she thought Ralph was mistaken. The current was still whirling at a fantastic rate, lapping now and again over the side of the tank or up onto the low wooden platform to trickle beneath Ralph's shoes. But as she strained forward to see, she suddenly realized the water was slowing. The merman, rather than pushing it along, now merely appeared to be floating with the current, the motion of his arms and tail sporadic, and frighteningly weaker.

Even so he was obviously alert enough to avoid the side of the pool where the Delano brothers stood. The brothers were lowering a slatted crate that vaguely resembled some kind of lobster trap into the water. Once they had the box in place, they picked up long, sharp poles and began herding the merman inside.

The merman refused to cooperate. Time after time he'd appear about to enter the crate, only to slip away at the last possible moment. For over an hour the game continued. Big Mike stayed in one place stabbing steadily, if ineffectually at the water, while Little Dougie chased about the perimeter, trying without success to prod the merman in the correct direction.

Obviously exasperated, Ralph had quickly grabbed a pole, too. From the platform, he tried to block their quarry from swimming from one end of the tank to the other, but the merman evaded the poles with seemingly little effort, almost appearing to taunt the men at times with a lazy flick of his tail before he agilely darted away.

Biting her lip, Beth remained resolutely at her vantage point, even though several of the jabs Ralph and Little Dougie directed toward the merman were vicious enough to make her wince. Ralph had told her father he'd be putting the merman in a smaller cage, and she could see he'd need to do so in order to get closer.

But then Ralph threw down his pole. "This is asinine—a complete waste of time," he snarled, wiping at the sweat on his face with the back of his hand. Even from a distance, Beth could see angry disgust in his expression as he added, "We're going to have to tranquilize him."

"No!" Beth cried out, jumping to her feet.

Everyone turned toward the staircase. Even the merman—a still, golden form in the water—glanced at her as she rushed down the stairs.

The Delano brothers and the merman continued to watch her descent, but Ralph turned away to climb down from the platform. When he reached the floor, he glanced at her, then looked over at Big Mike and Little Dougie.

"Take a break," he said, jerking his thumb in the direction of the stairs.

Without comment, the men threw down their poles and headed past Beth on their way out. Ignoring them, she hurried on toward Ralph. By the time she reached him, he was crouching next to a wooden trunk by the platform steps.

Beth, already breathless, grew even more so when she saw the dart gun he lifted out. "You can't!" she said.

He glanced at her, the recent anger on his face replaced with his usual expression of kindly wisdom. "I have to. He refuses to get into the cage."

"But there's no way to tell how a tranquilizer will affect him. It might hurt or permanently injure him."

"I doubt it, but even so that's a risk I'll have to take." Ralph rose to his feet, gun still in hand. He reached into the box again for some darts and stuffed them in his pocket as he reminded her, "I need to tend to that wound."

"But you said his wound was minor."

He shrugged. "I realized when I saw it again today that I was wrong. But don't take my word for it. See for yourself."

He gestured toward the platform, silently inviting her to climb up. Stung by the mockery in his tone, Beth glanced at his face. His expression was polite, concerned—and just the slightest bit condescending. Her fingers curled into fists. Ralph knew she was afraid of the water—not to mention the merman himself. But what he didn't know was that no Livingston ever backed down from a challenge.

Squaring her shoulders, she stomped toward the

wooden steps. Ignoring Ralph's surprised expression, she climbed up them, aware that he was following right behind her. When she reached the top, she gingerly walked out a few feet onto the platform, careful to stay in the center of the structure. There she paused, and forced herself to look out over the tank for the merman.

For a few dizzying seconds, she couldn't even find him. All she could see were the undulating peaks and valleys of the restless water. Then a golden flash broke the surface at the far side of the tank. Like a dolphin, the merman suddenly arced high into the air, droplets of water glittering all around him like a shower of diamonds before he disappeared back beneath the surface.

"He's never done that before!" Ralph exclaimed in surprise, then frowned. From beneath lowered brows, he slanted a considering glance at the woman by his side.

Beth barely noticed. Startled by the merman's sudden appearance, she'd only caught a glimpse of the red mark high on his left shoulder before he dived underwater. She kept her eyes on his shadowy form, waiting for him to resurface. When he rose into view again, he was much closer, and this time Beth saw his wound clearly. The sight made her stomach lurch. Obscenely red and raw, the gash looked painful—as if someone had crudely slashed a lightning bolt into the merman's smooth bronzed skin.

"It's ghastly," she said huskily as the merman dived back underwater. Turning to confront Ralph, she demanded, "You didn't see how bad it was yesterday?"

He shrugged, smiling ruefully. "All right, yes. I did. But I didn't want to worry your father."

"So you lied."

His smile faded, and his wide brow creased in a slight frown. Removing a dart from his pocket, Ralph slipped it into the gun before glancing at her again. His voice was very crisp as he retorted, "No, I simply bent the truth a little."

Snapping the clip down, he strode to the edge of the platform and peered into the water with a narrowed gaze. His jaw tightened as he saw that the merman had swum to the far side of the tank.

With an impatient exclamation, Ralph swung back around to face Beth. His frown darkening at the disapproval on her face, he added, "I'm concerned about your father's condition, too, Elizabeth. I thought it best to save him as much anxiety as possible. If you can't understand that—"

"I can," she interrupted, biting her lip.

He nodded abruptly. "Good. Now go get the Delanos back in here—and perhaps you'd better stay outside a while. This won't hurt the animal, but—"

Ralph broke off to stare down in stunned surprise at the strong, lean hand grasping his ankle. "What the hell is— Ack!"

The pistol flew into the air, skittering at Beth's feet as Ralph fell backward. With a huge splash he hit the water.

Beth's eyes widened and her hand flew up to cover her mouth. Good lord! The merman had jerked Ralph off his feet!

Hurrying to the end of the platform, she looked down over the edge. The merman was swimming away. Ralph was flailing just beneath the surface of the water.

He bobbed up, gasping for air. "Elizabeth! Get the Delanos, I—"

A muscular armed wrapped around his neck, choking the words off. The merman had circled, coming up behind him. With frightening ease, the merman pulled

Ralph back against his broad chest, holding him there with one arm across his throat, the other around his ribs. The immense muscles of the merman's shoulders and biceps leaped into corded knots beneath his gleaming brown skin as slowly, steadily, he tightened his grip.

Beth watched in horror as Ralph's eyes widened. His round cheeks turned from pink to red as he tore fruitlessly at the muscular forearm locked against his windpipe. His eyes rolled then bulged as he fought to escape, his expression filled with panic. But it was the sheer lack of emotion on the merman's face behind him that finally spurred Beth into action.

"Oh, no. Oh, please no," she pleaded unconsciously, desperately looking around, trying to decide what to do.

Her frantic glance fell on the tranquilizer gun Ralph had dropped on the wood. Snatching it up, she pointed it with a trembling hand toward the two figures battling in the water.

Ralph's struggles were growing feebler. His face, held just above the water line, turned from red to purple. On shaking legs, Beth moved to the other side of the platform, trying to get a clear shot at the merman's back.

She had it—his uninjured shoulder was in her sights. She steadied her hand. But a split second before she pulled the trigger, he swung around again.

The dart hit Ralph, high in the chest.

Beth's hand fell, the gun dropping from her numb fingers. She could see the dart sticking out from Ralph's wet shirt, right below the tanned forearm locked around his neck. The blood drained from her face. Now—thanks to her—the merman would finish Ralph off with no problem at all.

"Oh, God, no," she said, the words emerging huskily from her tight throat. "I've as good as killed him."

The thrashing figures suddenly became ominously still as trapped in the merman's hold, Ralph went limp. Over his shoulder, Beth's despairing gaze locked with merciless blue eyes. For a long, endless moment the merman stared at her silently.

Then he slid underwater, carrying Ralph with him. Beth's hand crept to her throat—then she gasped as a form suddenly burst out of the foamy water. Water flew everywhere as Ralph landed on the platform at her feet.

She quickly bent down over him. Water streamed from his hair, his clothes—dribbled out of his mouth and nose. He was soaked. He was weak. But when she pressed her fingers against the side of his neck, she could feel his pulse beating.

He was alive.

"Oh, thank you, thank you," she breathed, looking toward the water.

But the merman had glided away.

Chapter Four

Ralph obviously wasn't going to awaken anytime soon.

"The tranquilizer in that dart you showed me is pretty strong," Anne, her father's nurse, informed Beth about an hour later. The nurse straightened and stared down at the man in the bed, shaking her white head. "He'll probably regain consciousness in about six hours, possibly a little longer."

Bending over again, she lifted one of Ralph's eyelids and pointed a tiny flashlight at his pupil. Ralph didn't move at all. He continued to lie there with a silly grin on his face, as if he'd had a bit too much to drink.

Such a contrast to his usual demeanor, Beth thought, feeling oddly guilty. He was almost unrecognizable. The Delano brothers had stripped his wet clothes off after lugging him to his bedroom while she'd run to get Anne, but they hadn't bothered to dry Ralph before covering him with a sheet. A wet patch haloed his head on the pillow, and half of his red hair stuck out in greasy spikes, while the other half was plastered to his pale freckled skull.

The Delanos had laid him at a crooked angle on the mattress, too, Beth noticed. She kept wanting to straighten him out, as if doing so would straighten out this whole entire mess.

She watched Anne examine the puncture wound in Ralph's shoulder. The creases in the nurse's forehead deepened as she frowned at the tiny red mark, then glanced at Beth.

"You say you accidentally shot him while he was teaching you to use the dart gun?" she asked—for at least the third time.

"Um-hmm."

"And he acquired the bruises on his chest and neck when he fell?"

Beth nodded, still avoiding the older woman's eyes. She hated to lie to Anne. Over the years, the nurse had become more of an adopted aunt rather than simply her father's caretaker and, along with Captain McDugald, was one of the few people Beth considered a friend. Beth knew that Anne's snowy white hair, plump figure, and absentminded expression hid a very keen mind and equally kind heart.

Yet for some reason, keeping the merman a secret seemed even more important now than before he'd attacked Ralph. Perhaps because a normal merman was bad enough. A savage one was worse.

"Those don't look like bruises he'd get from a fall," Anne commented.

"He hit the edge of the platform after I shot him," Beth explained, trying to make her story a little more believable. Conscious that the other woman was watching her intently, she busied herself by pulling the sheet up higher over Ralph's milk-white chest. "But you think he's going to be all right?"

The nurse nodded. "He should be—barring any unforeseen complications," she added with characteristic caution. "He might have cracked a rib or two—without X rays I can't tell. He'll certainly want to take it easy for a week or so. But he's young, healthy. All he really needs to do right now is sleep it off." She turned away to repack her equipment in a small, brown case.

Beth gave a sigh of relief. If Anne said that Ralph was going to be all right, then she had no doubts he would.

The merman, however, was another story. A small frown puckered Beth's brow as she thought about the wound on his shoulder. "Anne…"

"Yes?"

"What would be the best way to treat a gash—say, from a piece of coral or even maybe a piece of wood or steel?"

Anne's gaze sharpened as she turned to scan Beth up and down. "Are you hurt?" she asked bluntly.

"No."

"Then who is?"

"No one exactly," Beth said, waving her hand in a vague gesture. "I was speaking hypothetically."

"I see." Anne raised her white brows questioningly. "And is this hypothetical gash infected? Does it need stitches?"

"I'm not sure—that is, I wouldn't think so." Good grief, Beth thought. She hoped not. "How would a person tell?"

"It needs stitches if that's the best or only way to stop the bleeding."

Beth gnawed on her lower lip, unsure if the merman's

wound had still been bleeding or not. "And if the bleeding has stopped?" she finally asked, hoping for the best.

"Then I'd possibly still administer antibiotics—and a tetanus shot wouldn't hurt either."

Beth nodded. Antibiotics in a pill form might be possible to get the merman to eat, but stitches or a tetanus shot had her stumped. She'd administered shots dozens of times at the children's care facility where Anne had persuaded her to donate time while in college, but giving one to the merman, well, good luck with that.

She was pondering the problem, when Anne interrupted her thoughts.

"Someone should stay with him until he wakes up." Anne snapped her medical kit shut with a decisive click, then looked back down at Ralph, who'd begun snoring loudly. "And I need to get back to your father."

Beth nodded. "I'll stay. Just give me a minute to change. Oh, and Anne— You won't mention anything to Dad or the captain about Ralph's accident, will you?"

"Not if you don't want me to," the nurse told her. "Frankly, I don't see a need to get Carl all worked up over it when Ralph will be just fine, and the captain isn't too fond of the young man as it is. He'll probably find a way to hold this against him for some reason."

"Thanks." Beth gave her a grateful smile, then left the room. She'd go change her clothes—their clammy dampness was becoming more uncomfortable by the second—then she'd talk to the Delanos, she decided. They could take care of the merman, while she stayed with Ralph.

It was a good plan. Except the Delanos wouldn't have any part of it.

"The pump and filtering device run just fine on their own. We're not going near that fish freak again,"

Dougie told her, spitting on the deck to emphasize his decision. Big Mike did, too, then smiled at her, his head bobbing in benign agreement with his brother's decree.

"Who knows when he'll grab one of us? We take our orders from Lesborn, not your father—or you," Dougie added, "and since Lesborn's out of commission…" He shrugged.

Beth looked from one to the other, seeing the fear beneath the sullen determination on Dougie's face and the bewilderment on Big Mike's. She straightened her shoulders. "Fine. You two take care of Ralph," she said decisively. "I'll take care of the merman."

Night had fallen by the time Beth returned to the hold. She'd settled the grumbling Delanos in with Ralph—ignoring Anne's look of surprise—then changed into a dress and had dinner as usual with her father, whose joyful expression and expansive plans about his "fantastic find" assured her he had no idea at all of what had transpired that day.

But as soon as the meal was finished, she slipped away, changing once again—this time into black shorts and a gray shirt. The dark clothing would help serve as camouflage, she thought, to prevent anyone noticing her going into the hold at such an unusual hour. And indeed, no one appeared to notice her as she hurried across the deck to the door.

After she unlocked it, she glanced carefully around, then slipped into the room, letting the door close quietly behind her. She paused, taking the time to twist the lock from inside. No way did she want anyone to come in unexpectedly and discover the merman. She had enough to worry about without that.

She started down the stairs, keeping a steadying hand

on the railing. The room was darker, more shadowy, than it had been earlier. Only a dark patch of sky was visible through the porthole. The lights along the wall were still on, though, and the powerful filtering pump hummed steadily. With all the uproar over Ralph, neither she nor the Delanos had remembered to dim the lights before leaving the room, Beth realized. They'd all been too upset—and just plain frightened.

She shuddered, remembering Ralph struggling in the merman's grip. Clutching the bag of medical supplies she'd ''borrowed'' from Anne a little tighter, she pushed the memory away and forced herself to continue her descent. Halfway down the staircase, she paused to look over at the tank. For once, the merman wasn't swimming around. For a few seconds, she couldn't even see him. He had to be in there somewhere, of course, but the surface of the water stirred gently, creating liquid shadows that made it hard to see.

Then she spotted him, lying with his forearms resting on the platform, the human half of his body lifted out of the water. His head lay on his arms, his face hidden in the crook of his elbow.

Beth's heart skipped a beat. Was he asleep? Unconscious? she wondered, as she hurried down the rest of the stairs. Surely he wasn't dead? Anxiety quickened her stride as she headed across the room toward the platform. He didn't move as she climbed the wooden steps, but as soon as she stepped out onto the structure, he lifted his head.

Relief flowed through her. No, not dead, not even unconscious. But definitely hurting. For a split second—before he'd assumed his usual expressionless mask—she'd swear she'd glimpsed suffering in those dark-blue eyes.

"You poor thing," she said involuntarily. She started toward him—then stopped in midstep as his lip curled, revealing excellent white teeth.

Beth remained frozen in place, uncertain what to do as he continued to watch her unblinkingly. She needed to get closer, to see to his shoulder. But she couldn't get her feet to move. From across the room, he'd looked formidable. Up close he was totally intimidating.

For one thing he appeared much larger than he had in the water. Nor, in spite of the hints of pain on his face, did he appear at all weak and helpless. Lying with his arms and torso propped on the wood made his shoulders appear broader, his brown chest deeper than Johnny Weissmuller's in the old Tarzan movies Anne so enjoyed.

But what really made Beth nervous was that unblinking gaze. Something in his unreadable, narrow-eyed stare made her pulse beat faster, kept her rooted in place like a person afraid of being bitten by a dangerous dog. Not that she'd ever had any contact with dogs—well, except for a puppy she'd played with once when *The Searcher* had anchored for a time near Catalina island. Nor was she exactly worried about being bitten—although the merman's teeth *did* look extraordinarily white and strong. No, she was much more concerned about being dragged into the water as he'd done to Ralph.

She couldn't forget how easily he'd held Ralph, or the strength it must have taken to throw the man—who had to weigh at least two hundred pounds—back up on the platform.

She took a deep breath trying to calm her racing pulse. The point to remember here was that he had thrown Ralph back, she reminded herself. He'd released him. If the merman was truly, knowingly vicious, then surely he wouldn't have done that.

Taking comfort from the thought, she took a tentative step forward—then paused again as his eyes gleamed in his shadowy face. Well, at least he'd stopped snarling. That was a good sign...wasn't it? Of course it was, she told herself. Maybe he just needed a few seconds to get used to her. To realize she wanted to help, not hurt him.

They continued to stare at each other as she tried to think of a way to get her goodwill message across. Maybe she should sing—that was said to soothe the wild beasts. It had worked with King Kong, hadn't it? She cleared her throat, preparing to try, then abandoned the idea. She really had a lousy voice. For all she knew, it might rile him up. Or at the least, send him underwater. Then she'd never get close enough to tend to his wound.

She tried a compromise, speaking in a soothing tone. "Now don't worry, I'm not here to hurt you," she said, slowly stepping toward him.

He didn't move, just continued to watch her. Taking this as an encouraging sign, she crept closer. "All I want to do is help you with that shoulder. I know it hurts you—it has to. But I have stuff here to help it heal. To make it feel better."

He still didn't move. She slowly inched forward until she was able to see his expression clearly. She drew in a breath as he turned his head slightly, and the light fell fully across his face.

No doubt about it, he was suffering all right. His dark, wet hair was slicked back from his face, emphasizing the strong cast of his features. Dark shadows lay beneath his deep-set eyes. His skin looked tauter across his high, proud cheekbones, his face leaner than it had before.

And even though his eyes were bright, his eyelids drooped heavily.

She drew closer still until she was within touching distance of his arm. Carefully, she crouched down and extended her hand. Slowly…slowly…until her fingers brushed his biceps.

He quivered…then went still.

Beth sucked in a breath, her eyes widening. Wonder and exhilaration flowed through her, and she wanted to laugh with the sheer joy of it. She was touching a *merman*—a mythical creature that wasn't even supposed to exist! Yet, how real—how solid he felt beneath her hand.

Gently she stroked his skin, enthralled by the sensations coursing through her. Her father had tried to explain to her once about the excitement of touching a gray whale—those giants of the deep who, after centuries of enmity with man, had recently begun allowing humans to stroke them in a lagoon off Baja.

But nothing—nothing compared to *this*, Beth thought, delicately trailing her fingers back up over the sculpted curve of his biceps. How smooth, yet firm his skin was. How rock hard the muscles beneath it. The most amazing thing of all was that he hadn't moved away.

She stroked his arm again, more lingeringly this time. A faint tremor ran along the taut muscle beneath her fingertips, and afraid he might swim away, she began talking again. "How handsome you are," she praised him, in that crooning tone that had worked so well before. "You're such a good-looking merman."

Beneath her palm, she felt him stiffen. His eyelids flickered, and he shot her an almost startled glance, before he looked away again, his expression going blank.

But even this minute sign of response encouraged Beth. She tried more compliments, getting into the spirit of the thing, pouring lots of enthusiasm into her voice. "So big and strong. So manly. And so warm…"

Her voice trailed off. "Maybe too warm," she added in a worried tone, a small frown creasing her brow.

She slowly lifted her hand toward his face. He sent her another sidelong glance and she said softly, "It's okay, it's okay. I'm not going to hurt you. I'm just afraid you might have a fever."

She gently brushed back his hair, combing her fingers through the damp, silky strands. She did it again, watching his thick dark lashes drift down with the movement, as if he were half-asleep. Then she placed her palm firmly against his forehead. He only allowed the contact for a few seconds before pulling away, but that was plenty long enough for Beth to make her diagnosis.

"You're so hot!" she exclaimed, dismay filling her voice. She sat back on her heels to look into his face. Sure enough, examining him more closely, she could see a slight flush beneath the dark tan on his cheeks. "You do have a fever!"

She moved to the side, leaning over him to see his back. She sucked in a breath as she stared at his wound. "And no wonder," she said huskily.

The jagged, lightning-bolt gash was dark red and swollen along the edges. But at least it wasn't bleeding, Beth noted, grateful for small favors. The skin had even begun to seal, forming a thick, uneven ridge that made her wince.

"It looks bad," she told him, unconsciously patting his arm comfortingly as she spoke. "But not as bad as it could be. The salt water must be good for it."

Of course he didn't respond; she knew he couldn't understand her. He just continued to regard her with that inscrutable stare. Beth continued to talk to him anyway, as much to calm her own anxiety as his. "You're going to have a terrible scar, but you already have a few anyway, don't you?" she added, as her gaze roamed over his chest and back.

This close, she could see other marks on his bronzed skin. One thin, faded white line ran beneath his well-defined pecs and the glinting silver medallion he wore. Another small scar was centered on his muscular back. Almost hidden beneath his hair she noticed another mark, curving from beneath his ear toward the back of his neck. She looked at it more closely, and with a slight jolt, saw it wasn't a scar at all, but a gill.

The realization shocked Beth—yet, it oddly reassured her, too. His rugged face, the hard muscles and warm flesh beneath her hand—his sheer, raw maleness—unsettled her in a purely female, human way. This new evidence of how different—how alien—he actually was, quieted the uneasy, feminine wariness that had unconsciously been stirring inside her.

She wasn't taking care of a strange man, but a strange animal, his features taut with mute suffering.

Her gaze returned to the injury on his shoulder. "Well, like I said, this one isn't pretty, but at least it's healing," she told him gently. "And it will heal even faster if you take this medicine I have for you."

She sat down cross-legged on the wood. Picking up the bag she'd brought, she began rummaging through it. "I have aspirin, an antiseptic cream and antibiotics."

He shifted slightly. Worried he was getting restless, she slanted him a quick glance. The silver medallion he'd strung around his muscular neck glinted against his tanned chest, catching her attention. The piece looked old, marked with some sort of ancient symbols Beth didn't recognize. Greek? Babylonian? Curiosity teased her for a second, then disappeared under the urgency of the task before her.

She lifted out one of the bottles. He'd stilled again, and seemed to be staring straight ahead. For a second, she thought he was looking at her thighs, revealed by her shorts. But then she realized he was staring at the vial in her hand.

She lifted the small white bottle higher, holding it in front of his eyes. "These are aspirin. As-pir-in," she repeated, sounding the word out and speaking louder, as if that might help him understand. "They relieve fever. Fee—ver. And the antibiotics—An-ti-bi-ot-ics—are for infection. See? They're just little pills." She spilled a couple out onto her palm. "Pink. Aren't they pretty? And they are good. S-o-o-o good."

She pretended to eat them, rubbing her tummy and smiling enthusiastically. "Mmm," she added, licking her lips.

His eyelids flickered again, but other than that, he didn't look too impressed by her performance.

Undaunted, she pretended to pour more into her hand and held them out. "Come on, fella. Just take them," she said, giving him a coaxing smile.

For a long moment, he simply stared at her mouth—then he looked down at her hand. Slowly, he bent his head forward. Beth held her breath as his warm breath caressed her palm, then yelped—jerking her hand away as he lightly nipped her fingers.

Her heart pounded. The pills and bottles went flying, dropping onto the platform. With a swipe of his hand, the merman flicked them off the wood and into the water. He glanced to the side, watching them sink, then returned his gaze to her face.

For once his expression was clear. Sheer satisfaction gleamed in his dark-blue eyes.

"Darn!" Beth shook her hand, adrenaline racing through her veins. His nip hadn't really hurt—but it sure had startled her. Her fingers still tingled. And now the pills were gone. She glowered at him as her pulse slowed again, but that only seemed to make his satisfaction increase. Her mouth tightened. "Okay, I had a feeling you'd be a tough case."

She picked up the bag again, aware that he watched with interest. She lifted it higher, so he couldn't see what she was getting out now. This time he didn't follow the movement. Instead, his gaze remained on her legs. Sliding restlessly up her knees, to her thighs and—

Quick as lightning, Beth struck. Bending forward she stuck the needle she had hidden in her hand into his arm, using the firm but fast technique she'd perfected at the care center.

For a second, the merman didn't even seem to notice the prick. Then his eyes widened—and narrowed. A growl rumbled in his throat.

Beth jerked the needle free, throwing herself backward as he lunged at her, his upper body coming farther up onto the platform as he grabbed for her feet.

She managed to elude him, scrambling backward like a crab. "I had to—honest," she said breathlessly, once she was sure she was out of reach. "Don't be upset. It's just a small shot—to stop you from getting sicker. It won't hurt you."

He didn't look appeased. His dark brows were lowered over his flashing eyes, and Beth hurriedly climbed to her feet to retreat even more.

She didn't stop until she was way back on the platform, as far away from him as possible. For a long, unnerving moment he continued to eye her, then he pushed back off the edge of the wood, dropping down into the water.

She breathed a little easier then, although her pulse skipped a beat when she glanced out over the top of tank and saw him watching her from the far side. Meeting his enigmatic gaze, she said earnestly, "I didn't mean to scare you, I just— Oh, don't leave—"

He slipped beneath the surface. Beth sighed—then gasped as with a sudden flip of his golden tail, he flung water in her face.

"That's not nice, darn it!" she fumed, wiping the salty wetness from her face with the edge of her shirt. Blinking the drops from her lashes, she looked out over the tank. "I said I was sorry!"

But the merman remained out of sight.

She'd touched him.

For a long time, he watched her blurry form from beneath the surface as she paced across the deck, calling softly, the damp curls of her golden-brown hair framing her earnest, heart-shaped face. It would have been easy to snatch hold of her, to carry her down into the water with him, but he resisted the temptation, biding his time.

Finally, she moved away. Silently, he rose to the surface. Remaining in the shadow of the platform, he watched her leave—her glinting hair rippling down her slender back like a waterfall, her pale legs moving with graceful ease as she slowly climbed the stairs. He didn't take his eyes off her slim figure until she disappeared through the door, shutting it behind her.

He listened until above the hum of the tank's motor and the quiet lapping of the water, he heard the lock spin with a faint clicking sound. Then he glanced away to stare unseeingly at the far side of the tank. The expression on his face remained as unrevealing as the smooth surface of the water in the small pool where they'd caged him. But deep inside—beneath the flesh that made him man, and the scales that made him mer—turmoil seethed.

He'd *never* been touched by a bare human hand before. He'd never allowed it. Even the three cretins who'd captured him hadn't done so. They'd wrapped him in a dirty tarp before hauling him onto the ship, and once they'd dumped him in their hidden pool, they hadn't touched him at all. The small, dark-skinned one had been too shrewd to make such an attempt; the bigger one too scared and stupid. Only the red-haired leader—the one called Ralph—had had the arrogance to try.

The spineless poltroon had planned to kill him. Or at the least, to render him unconscious. He'd heard him earlier in the morning brag to the others that he'd soon have "the beast" subdued; boasted of the riches he would receive two weeks hence, when he displayed their "find" to others. The merman shifted in the water, his expression hardening. Had the redheaded coward seriously believed he wouldn't fight? That he wouldn't recognize the danger of the weapon, the pistol Ralph had held in his hand?

No, of course Ralph hadn't known. The dirt dweller considered him to be no more than a dumb animal, without the ability to reason or react.

And obviously, *she* believed the same.

The merman's jaw tightened. An almost imperceptible twitch of his powerful tail caused the water to ripple across the tank. She'd spoken to him as if he were an idiot—or a child. He thought of the simple, careful speech she used—the pity he'd glimpsed on her face.

His teeth clenched and his tail lashed again, harder this time. Another wave rose to slap against the side.

Summoning the cold control which had helped him survive in the savage seas, he stilled the movement. He buried his anger, not wanting emotion to interfere with the logical workings of his mind as he planned his escape.

Carefully, he reviewed her actions, ruthlessly calculating how they might affect his own. By coming back down here, she'd revealed that she had no true awareness of the immense willpower it had taken not to kill this man Ralph while he had him in his grasp. She obviously thought he'd either spared the red-haired male by chance or maybe—his mouth twisted with cynical amusement at the thought—out of simple "human" kindness.

She didn't realize he'd thrown Ralph at her feet to serve as bait.

His eyes remained cold, but a small smile edged his lips. The ruse had worked. One small offering had reeled her in. She'd still been fearful, still cautious as she'd climbed up on the wooden dock over the tank, but her guard had already lowered a little. Her wary green eyes had darkened to a shadowy blue when she saw him; had held a softer light when they'd met his this time. She'd wanted to help—or at least, she hadn't wanted him to suffer unduly. So she'd returned with her pills and her potions. She'd crooned sweet, soothing words as she'd crept to his side. And then...she'd touched him.

He stirred restlessly, and forced himself to stillness once again. He wanted to tell himself he hadn't intended to let that happen. That the heated lethargy caused by his wound had blurred his thinking, slowed his reactions.

But that would be a lie.

Her nearness had weakened him somehow. When

she'd crouched next to him, she'd been so close that he'd felt the warmth from her body, her soft sigh against his skin. His flesh had tingled with an excitement that had flowed swiftly through him, tightening his muscles, arousing his curiosity. His breath had come faster, deeper, as he inhaled the scent of her. A far different, sweeter scent than any he'd smelled before but definitely female—definitely *her*. Caution had disappeared and he'd allowed her to touch him with her small, slim hands.

Involuntarily, his muscles quivered at the memory. His eyelids drifted half-shut. How cool her slender fingers had felt against his cheek. How gently she'd placed her soft palm against his forehead. He'd been so hot. The fever from his wound had seemed to burn more fiercely by the hour. But her touch had soothed the fire. Enough to let her stroke his arm, his shoulder. To run her fingertips through his hair.

A longing had built to touch her in return. To trace the tender curves of her pink lips, the arch of her slim eyebrows. To weigh the soft roundness of her breasts in his palms. To explore all the differences between them. The breeches she'd donned had been short, displaying her long, slim legs. He'd been able to see how smooth and pale her skin was, glowing with the same pearly sheen as the skin on her face and arms. He'd had to fight the urge to slide his hand up along her soft thighs to discover the hidden, female mysteries beyond.

The sight, the sound, the scent of her had distracted him. Taking him off guard. Giving her the opportunity to prick him with the tiny spear she'd hidden in her hand.

His eyes narrowed thoughtfully. He didn't feel drowsy, or inclined to go to sleep as the red-haired coward had done. Already the fire in his body was lessening, his mind growing clear once more. It appeared her claim was true that the little spear wouldn't hurt him. Mayhap she'd also spoken the truth when she'd said she wanted to help him; that the kindness in her touch hadn't been a lie.

He shifted, turning the possibility over in his mind, weighing all it might mean, what he might salvage if it was so. He would escape—that was certain as long as the sun shone in the heavens—but if she could be persuaded to help... His muscles tensed as hope surged. Ah, then he might do so unscathed! Live to see his people, see Pacifica once again.

Yet, if she lied...

Hope ebbed, dammed by caution. Nay, he could not take the chance of trusting her, not without understanding her better. The welfare of his people was at stake. Nor did he have much time to study the little female— just fourteen short days before this ship reached its cursed destination.

But he would spare a few, he decided, to determine if she might be friend, rather than foe. To lure her closer. Because either way, he would use her. She'd be his rescuer, his salvation.

Or the perfect hostage for his escape.

Chapter Five

All night long, Beth tossed and turned, unable to stop thinking about the merman. She hoped that the shot had helped him; she worried that it hadn't.

Although she'd gotten into the habit of sleeping in late with not much to do during the day except visit with her father, in the morning she rose early, anxious to check on her charge. Pulling on jeans and a blue sweatshirt, she thrust her feet into leather sandals and hurried through the cool morning mist to the hold. When one of the crewman passed her on his way to the galley, she greeted him briefly then stopped by the rail and pretended to watch the peachy sunrise. But as soon as the man was out of sight, she unlocked the hold and slipped inside.

Even before the door had closed behind her, she knew the merman was feeling better. From the top of the staircase she could see the water swirling in the tank, sloshing over the sides as he swam around and around.

Beth clung to the metal railing a second, feeling almost dizzy with relief. She took a deep breath to steady herself and watched him for a while, awestruck at his power and speed as he raced around the tank, fascinated as always by the sight of his glittering gold tail.

He slowed after a few minutes. Then, still unaware of her regard, rose waist high in the water. He maintained the pose without apparent effort, looking for all the world like a man standing up in a shallow pool—rather than in a tank over twenty feet deep. When he lifted his hands to slick his hair back from his face, Beth's admiring gaze traced his sculpted biceps before roaming over his chest. The skin there was smooth and bronzed, but dark hair marked his armpits and traced a faint line beneath his navel to disappear beneath the water.

She hastily looked away, feeling oddly embarrassed. It seemed such an intimate thing to notice—and such a masculine, human trait for him to have.

She left the hold quietly, not wanting to disturb him needlessly, her thoughts troubled as she headed for her father's stateroom. It was so confusing, trying to care for a creature who looked half-man, half-fish. Apparently, the merman's wound was better—which was a major relief—and she knew the powerful pump and filter kept the tank clean and full of oxygen. But there were other things she just wasn't sure of. Like what to feed him? How often? Did he need fresh water to drink? Her father would be the best one to ask, she decided. He would know what she should do.

But as soon as Beth entered her father's room, she could tell—even before Anne gave her a warning glance—that he was in no condition to discuss the merman. His eyes were glassy with fever, and he kept dozing off, too tired to maintain even the pretense of a conversation.

Beth didn't stay long, and when she got up from the chair by his bed to leave, Anne followed her out into the corridor, shutting the door behind her so they could talk.

"What's wrong with him?" Beth immediately asked, worry and dismay in her voice. "Do we need to get him to a hospital? Should I tell Captain McDugald to head for the nearest port?"

Anne shook her head. "Now settle down, honey. He's just had a slight relapse of that flu virus. Putting him in a hospital at this stage would do more harm than good."

"Are you sure?"

"Positive," Anne answered firmly. "I just want to keep him calm for the next week or so. Give him a chance to recover his strength. He's been all stirred up the last couple of days, overexcited about something...."

The merman, Beth thought silently.

"Rest is what he needs right now, more than anything else."

Beth stared at the nurse, her heart feeling heavy. How terrible to think that the thing her father had wanted the most might very well kill him.

"Don't look so upset," Anne told her, giving her a quick, comforting hug. "I'll keep you informed in case his condition changes. He'll be fine, I promise."

Beth nodded and turned to leave. She certainly didn't want to endanger her father's health any further. So, since Carl was obviously in no state to advise her about the merman, that left only Ralph. He was, after all, supposed to be an expert in the care of sea animals.

"Come in, Elizabeth, come in," Ralph called out from his bed, in response to her knock and soft query. "I've been waiting for you to come see me."

With a guilty twinge, Beth realized that with all that had happened, she'd almost forgotten Ralph's recent ordeal. He was still in bed, still rather pale—and the room smelled strongly of mentholated ointment, she noted silently as she entered, but even so he looked much better than he had the day before. Back in control. He'd combed his red hair, parting it precisely down the center, and donned a pair of navy-blue pajamas that fit him neatly across the shoulders.

He beamed at her, gesturing for her to come nearer. "Ah, you're a more welcome sight than caviar on a cracker," he declared, stretching out his hand.

"Uh, thank you," Beth responded. Since he was still holding it out, she clasped his hand briefly. But when his thick fingers tightened around her own, she pulled gently but firmly away.

He wasn't pleased about her slight withdrawal; she could tell by his reproachful look. But his expression brightened as soon she sat down in the chair next to his bed. "You must have been worried about me," he said, reaching over to pat her hand.

"Yes, well…" Beth hesitated. "Anne told me you'd be all right." Ralph's frown reappeared, so she added hastily, "How are you feeling?"

"My head aches tremendously," he said plaintively, raising his hand to his brow. He gave her a coaxing look from beneath his pale red lashes. "Rub it for me, won't you, cream puff?"

Beth suppressed the urge to grimace. Cream puff? She didn't think so. "Aspirin would be better," she said diplomatically.

Picking up the bottle on the nightstand by his bed, she tipped a couple of the pills into her palm. "Here, take these."

Giving her an almost baleful look, Ralph tossed them in his mouth, then downed the glass of water she offered next.

Beth sat back in her chair, and linked her hands in her lap. "Ralph, I was wondering..."

"Yes, sweet cakes?"

"About the merman—"

"I don't care to discuss that—that savage," Ralph declared, his face hardening. He lay back against the pillows, rubbing his forehead. "I'm just lucky he didn't kill me outright."

"Yes, I think you are," Beth agreed, before she could stop herself.

Ralph's lips thinned, but he conceded in an acid tone, "Yes, well, you did try to warn me he was dangerous. Obviously, you were right."

"Actually I'm not so sure about that," she said, smoothing a hand over a crease in her jeans. "When I went back down to see him last night—"

"You went down there again?" Ralph interrupted, sitting bolt upright on the bed. "After he attacked me?"

Beth nodded. "I had to. His injury looked infected— you told me yourself how bad it was. I knew I had to give him some antibiotics, so I did. In fact..." Unable to keep the news to herself a second longer, she blurted out, "I touched him."

"*You what?*"

"I touched him. I stroked his shoulder, his arm."

Ralph stared at her in astonishment. "Are you crazy? What did your father say about that?"

Beth stiffened a little at his tone, then forced herself to relax again. "Father doesn't know," she admitted. "He's not feeling well and Anne doesn't want him excited. I haven't even told him about your accident—"

"Or that you've been visiting the merman unsupervised," he interjected. "It isn't a safe thing to do, Elizabeth," he continued coldly. "Being all alone with that creature. I want you to stay away from the hold altogether from now on."

Beth widened her eyes in surprised protest. "But I can't. Someone has to take care of him. You're hurt and the Delano brothers are afraid to go near him."

"I'll deal with the Delanos," Ralph said, looking grim.

"No, don't. It's okay. I think the merman's beginning to—to trust me," she added almost shyly.

If she thought that would appease Ralph, she was wrong. His frown only deepened, and his gaze narrowed on her face.

Deciding to ignore his reaction, Beth said, "The only problem is...well—" She frowned thoughtfully. "What should I feed him? What does he like?"

"I wouldn't know."

Beth glanced at him questioningly. "What do you mean, you wouldn't know?"

For a second, Ralph didn't answer. Then he said curtly, "Actually, we hadn't yet fed him before the attack. Now, don't get excited—" he said, exasperation plain in his tone as he saw her stunned expression. "There's a reason for my decision. I decided to withhold food to make him more amenable."

"To weaken him, you mean."

"Are you questioning my methods?" he asked sharply. "You saw how he almost drowned me. How strong he is. Why, he cracked one of my ribs. I can barely move I'm so sore."

"He'll die if he doesn't eat," Beth pointed out. "And

besides, you went after him first—it's not his fault you got hurt. I also saw him throw you to safety.''

"And I suppose it wasn't *your* fault I was knocked out by the dart gun.''

Beth stiffened at the injustice of the remark. "I was trying to help you.''

"I know, I know,'' Ralph conceded, waving his hand in a dismissive gesture. He heaved a sigh. "All this hub-bub over nothing.'' His moustache turned up in a cajoling smile. "Why are we even fighting?''

"Because you want to starve the merman into submission,'' Beth said. "And I refuse to do that.''

"I'm only thinking of your welfare, Elizabeth.''

"My welfare? What does that have to do with starving him?''

Their gazes locked. "Fine,'' Ralph said stiffly. "I'm certainly in no condition to stop you from seeing him. But I'll have the Delano brothers cover the midnight and 4:00 a.m. checks on him so you don't have to go down there late at night. And, since your father put me in charge of this project, I would appreciate daily reports from you.''

Beth nodded. "All right.'' She got up to leave and headed for the door. She was reaching for the knob when Ralph spoke behind her.

"And I just want to make one thing clear, Elizabeth. If anyone gets hurt—the creature injures himself or someone else—then it's on your head, not mine.''

That statement kept echoing in Beth's mind as she made her way back down into the hold a little while later. The weight of it felt heavier on her shoulders than the bag of food in her arms. She wasn't concerned about the merman hurting anyone—staying out of his reach would prevent that. But how could she watch over him?

She'd never been responsible for the welfare of a living creature before—not a puppy, or a kitten. Not even a goldfish in a bowl. Yet, here she was, the primary caretaker of the only merman that anyone in recent history had ever seen. Possibly, the only one that existed. The realization was almost overwhelming.

Her spirits lifted, however, when she saw the merman was still swimming around.

"Oh, you must be feeling better," she exclaimed. "That shot did you some good, after all."

To her surprise, the merman halted at the sound of her voice. He turned his head to look at her, almost as if he were listening and trying to understand.

Excited by the thought, Beth hurried up the platform steps, adding, "I have something here that will help you even more. Food."

He swam closer as she walked out on the wood. "I'm sorry they've let you go hungry so long, and I hope there's something in here you'll like. Fresh fish would be the best choice, of course," she admitted, "but would you believe the chef said we don't have any? On a ship yet. So—"

She gasped, involuntarily recoiling as the merman suddenly planted his hands on the edge of the platform and raised himself out of the water. Like he had the day before, he lowered his powerful chest on the wood, the scaled part of his body draping down into the water. Resting his chin on his crossed forearms, he stared at her.

Beth stared back. Swallowing to ease the dryness in her mouth, she said shakily, "You must be hungry!"

He returned her wide-eyed look with his usual impassive expression, and after a few seconds, Beth's pulse slowly returned to normal. In his present position, he looked so—so human. Just a guy with a great build, taking a break during a vigorous swimming workout for a brief chat. Or in this case, a snack. But remembering how he'd tried to grab her the previous day—as well as Ralph's harrowing experience and gloomy warnings— she prudently remained out of reach as she spread out a tablecloth on the wood.

"Anyway, as I was saying, the chef is going to bake me—well, you—actually he's going to bake both of us, some halibut for dinner. But right now, I thought we'd try a few other things I managed to sneak out while he wasn't looking." She sat down on the cloth, and crossed her legs. Pulling the bag across her lap, she began rummaging through it. "Like vegetables."

She lifted out plastic bags of lettuce, broccoli and carrots and regarded them a little doubtfully. "Something in here should appeal to you," she told him, with more hope than conviction. "Think of them as land-grown seaweed."

Deciding lettuce looked the most seaweedlike, she put it on a platter and cautiously slid it toward him.

He pushed the platter back to her.

She repeated the action.

He did, too.

Beth huffed out her breath in exasperation. "This isn't a game we're playing here! You're supposed to eat this stuff. Watch."

Picking up a leaf of lettuce, she ate it—but without much hope that he'd do the same. After all, he hadn't followed her example with the pills.

But to her delight, when she pushed the plate over to him again, he bit a piece of lettuce, too—or rather, he ripped it apart with his white teeth, and chewed and swallowed rapidly. He quickly finished off all the lettuce there was, then shoved the platter back over to her again, watching her intently.

She smiled. "All right—we're making progress here. Try a carrot."

She bit a carrot, then passed some over to him. He bit one, too—and spat it out again on the wood.

"Well, yuck…" Beth made a face. "A simple 'No, thank you' would have sufficed. But okay—you made your point. Obviously carrots aren't your thing."

Neither were broccoli—or tomatoes. He spat those all out, too.

But when she offered him some caviar—after following the now established routine of tasting it first—he eagerly scooped it up with his fingers and downed it in a few huge gulps.

"Goodness. I can't believe you like that stuff so much. Tastes terribly salty to me," she said, sitting back on her heels to watch him. As soon as he finished, she opened another jar of caviar. If anything, he ate this one even faster than the first. Then he pushed the empty platter back to her, obviously waiting for more.

"Yes, well, I don't have any more," she told him, apologetically. "Now, don't look at me like that—" she protested, as his eyes began to narrow. "How did I know that you'd go crazy for the stuff? In fact, if Ralph hadn't mentioned it, I wouldn't have thought of caviar at all." She reached for the bag again. "But don't worry. I have something that I'm sure you'll like even better." Triumphantly, she lifted a can from the bag and turned the label toward him. "Ta-da! Mermaid food!"

There on the side was a cute drawing of a little mermaid, holding a wand and smiling happily to show how delicious the tuna inside was.

The merman blinked. Then, with an almost disbelieving shake of his head, he glanced away.

Disappointed at his reaction, Beth glanced at the label herself. It seemed pretty self-explanatory to her. She looked back at the merman.

"It's tu-na," she said, unconsciously using the slow and distinct diction that seemed appropriate when explaining something to him. Picking up the can opener she went to work. "Chick-en-of-the-sea," she elaborated when the lid popped off. "Not that it tastes like chicken. But you've probably never had chicken, so that really doesn't matter."

She scooped the fish onto the platter, and dutifully tasted a bite. But the merman wouldn't eat the tuna, shoving it back to her with every indication of disgust. He was, Beth discovered during the remainder of the day as she trotted back and forth to the galley, a very picky eater.

"He ate the fish that Chef Pierre baked," she told Ralph late that evening, when she dutifully paid him another bedside visit to report as promised. "But only after I accidentally spilled salt all over it. I think that might be why he likes your caviar so much," she added thoughtfully as she considered the matter. "Because it's so salty."

"You fed him my beluga!" Looking pained, Ralph lifted his hand to cover his eyes. "He'd probably be satisfied with chum."

"I doubt it. He wouldn't even try tuna," Beth said crisply. "So unless we run out, caviar or baked fish is what we'll give him."

With a resigned sigh, Ralph lowered his hand again to give her a questioning glance. "Did Pierre suspect anything?"

Beth shook her head. "No, he thought the fish was for me. I did notice one of the men giving me a strange look when I went down with more food around lunchtime," she admitted reluctantly. "But I told him I was taking notes on the behavior of a dolphin that you'd captured, and that I'd decided to have a snack while I watched. That seemed to satisfy him."

"Well, I'm still not satisfied with you taking such chances—endangering your life by going near that creature. Believe me, I know the signs of rogue male when I see one," Ralph stated grimly. "Every species has them. He's too unpredictable to be trusted. He'll never be tamed."

Beth frowned, turning that over in her mind. "I'm not sure that's true. He did let me touch him," she reminded Ralph. "And at times, he is predictable. For instance, he won't eat anything unless he's seen me try it first. It's almost as if—" She paused, groping to explain. "As if he's having me test it. Like he thinks it might be poisoned or something."

Ralph snorted in disbelief. "Huh! What he's doing is called simple mimicry—a basic animal reaction. To put it in layman's terms," he added, in that condescending tone that always made her grit her teeth, "monkey see, monkey do."

Beth didn't argue; she knew nothing she could say would change Ralph's mind. Yet, she was secretly convinced that the merman was much more intelligent than they realized.

Oh, she could understand why Ralph might not believe it, she thought later that night as she sat on the platform watching the merman swim. His expression was so blank—like Big Mike's, she thought, then frowned over the comparison. No, that wasn't quite right. Big Mike's facial muscles were lax, contributing to his habitual vacant look. With Big Mike, you knew the clock tower was empty.

But the merman's facial muscles were tight, controlled. As if he willed himself to sustain that unrevealing mask. At times, as he watched her, his expression would seem to alter somehow. Behind his eyes, she could almost sense something ticking, like a time bomb waiting to explode. Whenever that happened, she'd feel restless, sort of quivery inside. It made her careful to remain out of his reach.

Yet, she grew less cautious, less afraid, every hour she spent with him. Except for a brief visit to check on her dad, she spent the whole next day down in the hold. She fed the merman—who still silently insisted she try each meal first—and watched him swim. She also tried to communicate with him.

At first, she started by trying to teach him to recognize—and possibly respond to—a few simple words. Like *wa-ter,* and *tank,* and *mer-man.* But the merman had no interest at all in the lessons. He'd yawn, or swim away. And invariably he'd splash her.

Beth simply hated that—but she hated giving up even more. She went and got a supply of tank tops and shorts from her room, and stuck them in the large supply closet where Ralph stored his work clothes. Stubbornly, she'd change and begin the lessons anew, tying back her wet hair and marching back toward the tank determined to succeed. But when the merman splashed her for the third time in one hour, she'd finally had enough.

"Quit it!" she told him, her hands clenched by her sides, water streaming down her face as she stared at him from the platform. "There's no reason for you to behave like that. I'm just trying to—"

She paused, struck by a sudden realization. She certainly had his full attention now! He floated near the platform, his eyes bright and gleaming as he watched her from the water. He'd listened to her at other times, too, when she'd simply talked to him. Maybe a conversational tone, the constant flow of her voice, would work better at getting through to him and keeping his attention, than repeating single words.

Testing her theory, she began talking to him constantly. She didn't worry about what she said, but sat on the platform and rambled on about whatever came to mind for the rest of the afternoon.

At first she stuck to general topics—world politics, religion, the latest fashions—whether skirts would get longer or shorter in the fall, what colors would be in style. By the next day, she'd moved on to more personal concerns and interests. How far the ship still had to go to reach port in San Diego, past voyages she'd been on, places she'd seen. How much she'd enjoyed her college classes in sociology—learning about different people, different cultures—before she left to be with her father.

And her new program appeared to be working. The merman didn't yawn, or splash her, or swim away once. He stayed close to the platform, his attention fixed on her face. He was, Beth decided, a fantastic listener. It was a pleasure to talk to someone who wasn't preoccupied with his own thoughts like her father, always worried like Anne or constantly lecturing like Ralph. The merman simply listened, not agreeing or disagreeing with anything she said.

"Which, more than anything else, proves how unlike a real man you are," Beth told him.

Her muscles felt stiff, so she stretched, twisting from side to side, then reaching up as far as she could before lowering her arms again. She'd been sitting on the platform for more than three hours that morning, talking to him—searching for the merest hint of response in his face—as he lounged nearby in the water.

Lifting up the edge of her shirt, she wiped off a trickle of sweat at her temple. Even in her thin pink tank top and matching shorts, she felt hot. The late-summer storm that had been threatening was moving in from the south. It wouldn't catch *The Searcher* for a few days yet, but the patch of sky in the porthole had a leaden cast, and the air in the hold was heavy and humid.

She shifted out of the path of the sunlight beating down from the porthole overhead, and lifted her hair to cool her nape. Catching a movement from the corner of her eye, she glanced at the merman. He was still watching her, but his expression had shifted to that "other" look—the one that made her stomach clench then go all quivery inside.

Her muscles tensed. She dropped her hair, preparing to rise, but then he glanced away. His eyelids drooped, half shielding his gaze for a moment, and when he looked at her again, the expression was gone.

With a sigh, Beth settled back down. She noticed he was silently lashing the water with his tail—a sign, she'd discovered during the past two days, that he was either about to splash her or start on another round of his endless swimming. She started talking again before he could do either.

"Dad knew you existed—that we'd find you," she told him, leaning back on her hands and stretching out her legs, pleased when he went still again. "Not you specifically, of course, but certainly mermaids. He saw one over twenty years ago and refused to give up the hunt ever since."

"He's like that," she confided. "Kind of an obsessive-compulsive personality. It's what made him so successful as a scientist—the way he could focus on something and never give up."

She heaved a sigh and changed position again. Drawing her legs up against her chest, she wrapped her arms around them and rested her chin on her knees. "The only trouble is, now that he's accomplished this goal—he'll probably turn his attention to his second major concern—" She made a wry face. "Marrying me off. He wants grandchildren, you know. The reassurance that when he's gone, his fortune and his DNA will continue on in future generations. He's especially anxious to see it happen soon because he's so sick."

She looked down at her feet, revealed by her strappy sandals, and critically examined the garnet polish she'd selected. "I want to get married, of course. And the guys in college and in the ports we visited, were nice enough I suppose, but when it came to getting serious…"

She shrugged. "Well, take Trevor, for instance. Good hair and teeth, a pretty decent build—maybe not in your league," she conceded, surveying the merman's wide shoulders, "but not bad. Basically, an all-around good-looking guy. Anyway he takes me out dancing—we have a good time, and then, when we get back into his sports car he yanks me into his arms and starts kissing me. He wasn't bad, I suppose…if you enjoy having a big lug try to tickle your tonsils with his sloppy wet tongue." She wrinkled her nose. "Yuck! Well, anyway, the point is I just can't see what all the hoopla is about."

She shot the merman a quick glance then studied her toes again. "The thing is, I always thought—hoped— I'd meet someone I'd really click with. Someone who laughs at the same things I do, thinks the same way. Someone who, you know—turns me on.''

The silver ring on her little toe glinted in the light. She wriggled her toes to make it shine again, then ran her finger over the thin metal, cast in a pattern of tiny waves.

"Maybe it's me. Maybe I'm just not a very sexual person." She mused on that for a few minutes, then looked over at the merman again, meeting his eyes. "Maybe I should just accept that and go with Dad's choice. After all, he believed in Dad when no one else did. And even though he may act rather stern—okay, even pompous at times—at least Ralph is a gentleman. And I know he's interested in me—"

She broke off in midsentence as something dangerous moved behind the blue gaze locked with hers. The merman's expression seemed to harden. The muscles in his neck and powerful shoulders corded and grew taut.

Beth's eyes widened, then narrowed. She gazed intently at the merman's face as she tried to decide if there actually had been a change in his demeanor or if she'd simply imagined it.

"What is it, fella?" she asked softly. "Is your shoulder hurting you? Are you hungry?"

Again, a fleeting shade of some indefinable emotion crossed his face. Impatience? Pain? Beth couldn't be sure, but she'd swear there was a brooding intensity in his eyes that hadn't been there before.

"Just tell me," she urged.

His lips parted—and her heart skipped a beat. She held her breath, then released it with a sigh as he suddenly dived underwater. Beth watched his golden form glide beneath the surface, thinking how ridiculous she could be—imagining he'd wanted to tell her something; that he'd been trying to speak.

Yet, for the rest of the day, his behavior continued to worry her. There was a distant look in his eyes, an aloofness in his hard features, that she hadn't noticed before. Nor did he swim around the tank for long. Instead, he remained in the shadows, as far from the platform as he could get.

At first, she thought that maybe he was simply hot, too. She'd seen him glance sometimes at the sun shining down through the porthole, and he never came up on the side of the platform where the light landed directly. But as the day wore on, she became more and more convinced something was wrong and by late afternoon, she was seriously alarmed.

Hunger wasn't his problem. He ate the food she offered after their usual ritual of her tasting it first, but his lack of enthusiasm made her worry even more. He didn't seem sick; his face wasn't flushed and she knew his wound was healing nicely. What was the problem?

She watched him as he lingered in the shadows. Something about his solitary figure, the brooding look on his face, gave her a possible answer. Was he—could he possibly be—lonely?

"Is that the problem, boy? Are you lonely?"

He turned his head away, for once not even bothering to look at her as she spoke.

Beth sighed. "Well, I know what that's like. It's no fun, is it."

She looked down into the water, watching the bubbles froth up from the jets on the pump. "I can't remember a time when I haven't felt alone—at least, not since my mom died. Even at boarding school I didn't quite fit in.

True, I was rich, which helped a little, but on the other hand my father was considered crazy, which didn't.

"I don't have too many friends now, either," she admitted softly. Even so, she was better off than the merman. At least she had her father, and sweet, motherly Anne to confide in. And old Captain McDugald seemed gruff, but Beth knew he cared about her, too. And of course she had Ralph who—well, was Ralph. "But you have no one to keep you company, do you, boy? Day after day, swimming around all alone."

The more she thought about it, the more convinced she became that loneliness was his problem. After all, he'd lived in the ocean—with millions of fish all around. Now he was stuck by himself in a tank.

The idea bothered her so much that instead of going to Ralph's room after dinner to give him a report, she returned to the hold, carefully carrying a fish in a bowl.

"It's one of Ralph's specimens," she told the merman. He was still at the shadowy side of the tank, but he lifted his head to stare at her as she cautiously climbed the platform steps, holding the bowl in front of her so it wouldn't spill on her jeans or white blouse.

He continued to watch as she set the bowl down on the edge of the platform. "I got it out of the lounge where he keeps his collection. Dougie was fixing the filter in this one's aquarium, and I thought it was the perfect opportunity to bring the fish down to visit you for a little while."

Her plan appeared to be working. The merman left the spot he'd stayed in all afternoon to circle closer. After a couple of seconds of this cautious reconnoitering, he glided over to the platform. Planting his hands on the wood, he hoisted himself up, his lower body remaining in the water as usual. Resting his chin on his crossed forearms, he stared at the fish.

Delighted with his reaction, Beth crouched down and pushed the bowl a little closer so he could see the fish better. "He's some kind of piranha," she said confidingly. "Very rare and very, very expensive, according to Ralph. Really vicious, too. Which is why he can't be put in with the other fish. He'll kill them. He'll even bite a person's finger off if he gets the chance."

To demonstrate, she put her finger against the bowl. The little brown fish's eyes bulged malevolently as he rammed the glass, jaws parted to reveal razor-sharp teeth. "See?" Beth said, as she did it again. "Pretty scary, huh?"

She sat back on her heels. The merman glanced at her, then lifted his hand. Reaching out, he touched the glass as she had done and watched the fish attack.

Beth smiled, pleased with the intent, interested look on his face. "I call him Nasty Ned—which reminds me..." She got comfortable, sitting down and crossing her legs. "We never gave you a name, did we?"

She watched him tease the fish. He was moving his long finger back and forth rapidly, whipping Nasty Ned into a frenzy of rage. "What about Golden Boy?" she said musingly. "Don't you think that's a good name?"

The merman's hand froze. Slowly, he turned his head to look at her.

"No, you're right," Beth conceded, meeting his eyes. "Makes you sound like a horse, doesn't it?"

She frowned and hugged her knees, thinking harder. "What about Moby Dick? Or Flipper? Maybe Willie— No, wait! I've got it!" She straightened up, snapping her fingers. "Waldo!" she declared. "I once read a wonderful romance with a fish named Waldo in it, who was really smart. Isn't that perfect? I bet even Ralph will like it!''

For a moment longer, the merman stared at her. Then he glanced back at Ralph's fish and suddenly reached into the bowl.

''No! Stop!'' Beth cried out. Horrified, she leaned forward to try to snatch the bowl away.

She was too late. With a quick movement, the merman grabbed the fish and popped it in his mouth. His strong white teeth ground together with a distinctly crunching sound—once, twice—then he swallowed.

Nasty Ned was history.

''Oh, no! How could you!'' Beth climbed to her feet to glare down at the merman. Shaking her finger at him, she scolded fiercely, ''*Bad* merman! Bad, *bad* merman!''

He sank out of sight beneath the water, abashed by her tone, Beth was sure—then suddenly he exploded up again, drenching her with a huge burst of water.

''Darn it, darn it, darn it!'' Beth held out her arms. She was drenched. Water poured down from her hair, her clothes, to puddle at her feet.

She put her hands on her hips. ''That's it. I give up. See if I ever try to help you again,'' she declared in disgust. ''You're certainly no Waldo! In fact, I think I'll go with Moby Dick—minus the Moby.''

She'd turned, and had taken two squishy steps toward the platform steps when a deep voice stopped her in her tracks.

''Not Dick,'' a baritone rumbled behind her. ''Saegar.''

Chapter Six

Beth slowly turned around. The merman was once again draped over the edge of the platform, his powerful arms casually crossed, supporting his weight as he stared up at her.

She met his eyes, knowing her own had to be wide with amazement. "I'm Beth Livingston," she responded automatically. "Did you—what did you say your name was?"

Had she imagined that he'd spoken? she wondered, as he simply regarded her with that unreadable expression she'd grown to expect. Just when she'd decided she must have been mistaken—that her mind was playing tricks on her—he spoke again, making Beth gasp so hard she almost choked.

"Saegar," he repeated, his voice slightly rough but richly timbred. "My name is Say-gar."

He pronounced the words slowly and distinctly, in the same manner she'd so often spoken to him. As if...Beth swallowed, feeling her face beginning to burn...as if he suspected she might not be too bright.

"You can *talk*," she said inanely, probably confirming his suspicion.

"Aye."

"All this time, all those hours I've sat there rambling on and you've never once uttered a word?" She thought of all the things she'd said, some silly, some personal, and her cheeks burned hotter with embarrassment and indignation. "If we'd known you could talk—"

"What, Beth Living Stone?" he asked as her voice trailed off. "You would have released me? Then release me now!"

"I want to...but it's not up to me." Beth turned on her heel as a thought occurred. "I'll go get Ralph. Once he learns that you can speak—"

"Nay!"

Once again, Saegar's voice stopped her in midstride. She turned back around again, and regarded him doubtfully. "Nay?" she repeated. "As in no?"

"Aye. Nay."

Beth frowned. He was certainly throwing a lot of ayes and nays around. "You don't understand. This changes everything. Ralph needs to—"

"If you tell him, I will not speak again."

Beth met his determined gaze. He meant the threat; there was no doubt about that. And he was just the kind of guy who could stick with it, too, she decided. After all, he'd already remained silent for almost a week. It would probably be no effort at all for him to do so forever.

But, oh, how she hated being the only one who knew something this important. How thrilled her father and

Ralph would be at the opportunity to talk with him, to get answers to all their questions.

She gave him an uncertain glance, trying to decide whether or not she could change his mind.

Despite the gravity of his situation, Saegar felt a tug of reluctant amusement at the expression on her face. The little female so clearly wanted to argue. Obviously, Beth Living Stone was not accustomed to taking orders, but rather to doing as she pleased.

But not in this matter, he thought, his amusement disappearing. He gave her a warning look. "You will tell no one, but simply release me yourself."

"Fine, I won't tell anyone," Beth agreed, albeit grudgingly. "But then neither can I release you. My father would be devastated if I did something like that behind his back."

Saegar's gaze narrowed on the stubborn jut of her small chin. He'd learned while listening to her how important her father was to her, how she feared hurting him. He also knew Ralph had convinced her that he—and his kind—were creatures without human emotions, human ties.

He studied her for a long moment, trying to decide how to convince her that he was neither fish nor beast as Ralph had called him; that she had no right to keep him against his will.

Words were the only weapon he had at the moment, he decided, so he'd best use them well. "Perhaps you will change your mind, once you understand about my people," he mused, thinking aloud.

Her face lit up. "So there are more like you? But where are they? Where do they live?" she asked, her voice breathy with excitement. "What happened—"

"Silence!" Saegar commanded, holding up his hand.

"I know *you* can speak, Beth Living Stone. I've listened to you do so these past two days. But if you truly seek the answers to these questions flowing from your busy tongue, then remain silent now and listen."

Well! Beth thought, lifting her eyebrows. It was great he could speak, but talk about bossy and demanding! Just because she wasn't as—as quiet as he obviously was, didn't exactly mean she had a busy tongue! She opened her mouth to defend herself—then snapped it shut as she caught the mockery in his gaze. Fine. She could be quiet when necessary.

Without a word she retraced her steps along the platform, and sat down, crossing her legs. Folding her hands in her lap, she assumed an expression of patient encouragement.

Saegar glanced at her, then slowly pushed away from the platform. He sank beneath the water then smoothly surfaced again, about ten feet away. Drifting back a few more feet, he propped his wet shoulders against the side of the tank and folded his arms across his chest.

He studied her expression, his own unreadable once again. But this time, Beth didn't feel that he was mocking her, but rather turning something over in his mind.

"My ancestors were once like yours, with legs to help them travel great distances across land to aid them in finding food and shelter," he finally began, the cadence of his rough voice slow and measured, as if he repeated a story he'd heard many times before. "But they didn't settle in the deep valleys or the rocky mountains but lingered instead beside the ragged edges of the shoreline. There they harvested the rich bounty of the waves—adding their strength to the strength of the tides to draw in their nets. And their labor caused the salt of their brows to fall into the ocean, and the oceans repaid them by spraying water back up over them to cool their skin.''

Absently, he unfolded his arms to run a hand across the surface of the pool, causing a ripple to follow in its wake. Scooping up a handful of water, Saegar let the sparkling drops spill from his cupped palm, as he added, ''Thus, in a thankful baptism of joy, they became a people of the sea.''

When the last drop fell, melting back into the pool, he crossed his arms again. ''And the restless sea beckoned them onward. Bid them come discover what lay beyond the horizon. So, my people built boats, and traveled the seven seas, until they found an island—vast and verdant, a green jewel in the ocean. There they settled, and there they thrived and flourished, creating a magical land of advanced culture and science. A world of untold wealth and ease. And they called the island...Pacifica.''

His voice lingered on the name, and the yearning in his husky tones seemed to reverberate within Beth, making her shiver. Drawing her knees up beneath her chin, she wrapped her arms around her legs, her gaze still fixed on Saegar's rugged face.

He'd forgotten all about her, she thought, seeing the faraway look in his eyes. Forgotten where he was. Instead of trapped in the dark hold of a ship, he was once again in Pacifica.

The silence stretched, broken only by the soft swishing sound of the water, lapping futilely against the tank and the soft hum of the pump. She hugged her legs tighter, wanting to say something, to try to comfort him somehow, but her small movement broke his reverie.

He glanced her way and started talking again. ''Then a volcano erupted and sank the island. But a large dome of earth covered Pacifica with a pocket of air that protected the people. And—despite the fear and hardship that followed—they slowly began to thrive and flourish once again. With the help of our best scientists, they also began to evolve. They developed gills to help survive in the water. Tails to help them swim—to propel them across the oceans a hundred times more swiftly than legs could carry a human across land. But these changes took time, and for centuries—millennia—the people of Pacifica were isolated from your kind. By the time we were capable of making contact once again, two factions had arisen in our land—Swimmers and Breathers—both at odds over whether to reunite with your world."

He swept out his left arm. "Breathers want reunification. They believe interaction with your kind will be good for our people. Exploration and expansion is their mantra, fearing that isolation will eventually destroy Pacifica."

He spread out his other arm. "Swimmers believe interacting with others is dangerous to our society. They urge isolation from the rest of the world." Meeting her eyes, he folded his arms again and threw out his chest to announce, "I am aligned with—"

"The Swimmers," Beth said before he could.

She shrugged apologetically as Saegar slanted her a reproving glance. "Sorry," she said. "I didn't mean to interrupt; it just slipped out." She couldn't resist asking, "But I'm right, aren't I?"

A shade of annoyance crossed his face. He nodded shortly, then lifted his head proudly. "My father is King Okeana, ruler of Pacifica and the leader of the Swimmers."

"I see…" Beth wrinkled her brow in puzzlement "…I think. But if the Swimmers believe in isolation, than what were you doing out in the ocean?"

"A war broke out between our people—between the Swimmers and the Breathers." He paused, and his voice roughened. "When my mother, Queen Wailele, was killed, my father decided he dare not risk his children. He sent my three sisters and me away in different directions, each with a guardian to protect us. I was six when we were sent into exile. Thalassa was eight. The twins, Phoebe and Kai were but babes of two."

Beth was dumbfounded. "You're kidding."

He raised his eyebrows. "Kidding?"

"I mean—never mind. It's just an expression." Beth stared at him, unable to believe a parent could do such a thing. "How could your father do that?" she asked slowly. "Send out babies to survive in the ocean?"

Saegar frowned. "My father did what he thought best for the safety of his people, as well as his children. And the girls would not have remained in the ocean for long," he added almost reluctantly. "Their guardians would have taken them to land. To hide amongst your people."

"To land!" Beth frowned in confusion. "How could they? I mean, their tails—"

She broke off. For some reason, mentioning their tails seemed rather rude. Still, she couldn't help adding, "Wouldn't they be noticed immediately?"

Saegar shook his head. "Nay. They would not. For mer—for most Pacificans, the transformation between land and sea is temporary. At a specific level of salinity, tails are grown to help with survival in the water. Back on land, the membranes subside. For most, their legs are once again exposed. Thus, they can move easily between land and sea, and while on land, appear completely human. Like you."

Idly amused by her astounded expression, he relaxed

a little, leaning back in the water. He lifted his tail fin to stroke the water lazily, then submerged it again, causing a fan of tiny ripples to spread across the pool.

She followed the movement before her gaze flew back to his, her eyes widening. "So you—"

"Not me," Saegar interrupted, his amusement fading. "I am not mer, but meremer—one of the cursed ones." His tail lifted and fell, hitting the water harder this time. "For me and others like me, there is no changing back and forth. We are…as we are."

"Cursed?" Beth's eyes widened again. "Like some kind of spell?"

He shook his head. "Nay, cursed at birth."

It must be some kind of recessive gene, she thought, that showed up in a certain amount of the population.

"How—" Sad, Beth almost said, but bit the word back just in time. The fierce pride in his rugged face made it more than clear that the sentiment would not be welcome. "Interesting," she murmured instead.

But how ironic that his father Okeana, a Swimmer who didn't want contact with humans, had been forced to send his children away from Pacifica to ensure their survival. She felt bad for Saegar, she really did. "Are there many like you? Many meremer?"

"A few. Bali, my guardian, was meremer also. He was a wise old man who knew well the ways of the sea—and your people also," Saegar added, his mouth twisting wryly as he threw a glance around the tank. "He taught me your language as he'd heard it from sailing ships but warned me to avoid dirt dwellers if I wished to make it safely home again."

Beth winced at the sarcasm in his voice and the term *dirt dwellers*. Appropriate, she supposed, but still rather insulting. "You were on your way home?"

He nodded curtly. "To reunite with my family."

"Oh." Beth grimaced again, giving him a guilty glance from beneath her lashes. "How late are you?"

"Ten years."

"What!"

"Ten years," he repeated tersely. "And I have not seen Pacifica—or my family—for over twenty-five. Unbeknownst to me, my father planned for us to return ten years ago, bearing the seals entrusted to us—" He lifted up the silver medallion around his neck. "This I but learned on Bali's death, three weeks ago."

"You mean for ten years your guardian basically lied to you—kept it a secret that you were due to go back?" Beth shook her head in outrage. "But why would he do such a thing?"

"I am not sure why," Saegar admitted. "Bali grew more and more distrustful of anyone—even other mer—as the years passed. He may have simply not wanted me to return into what he might have perceived as a dangerous situation." His stern expression grew even more bleak. "But he died before I could question him on the matter."

"So for all you know, your family has been waiting for ten years for you to return. They might even think you're dead." Her brows drew down in disapproval. "Well, I think what Bali did was terrible. No matter what his reason."

Saegar's jaw tightened, and his blue eyes flashed. "You dare to say this? You, who caused my capture with a siren's trick?"

"What are you talking about?" Beth exclaimed, surprised at his reaction. "I had nothing to do with your capture!"

"Aye, you did, Beth Living Stone."

"No, I didn't!" Beth insisted, unaccountably disturbed by his misconception. "I saw you out there, I admit, but I thought you were a fish. I had no idea they'd go after you—or any idea at all that you were a merman. All I've tried to do is to help you. To make sure your wound didn't get infected, that you ate. I'm not the one to blame—I'm not!" she declared, seeing the skeptical look in his eyes.

He shook his head, a stern expression on his face. "That is a lie, Beth Living Stone. You are the one who lured me into danger. With the ancient gestures of my people, you signaled for help from the bow of your ship."

Beth's mouth dropped open, then snapped closed. "What! I never did that!"

Saegar's expression darkened even more at her continued denial. His brows lowered over his narrowed eyes, as he demanded, "On the day of my capture, did you not stand on the bow of your ship and cover your mouth with your hands? Bow three times to the setting sun, then call to me, using the soft barks of a seal?"

Beth stared at him. "Are you crazy? Me? Bark like a seal? I don't know what—"

She sucked in a breath, her eyes widening as she realized what must have happened. Her hand flew up to cover her mouth. "Omigosh!" she muttered into her palm. She could feel heat rising in her cheeks. *Good lord, how embarrassing.*

Ignoring her burning face, she lowered her hand again to explain. "I wasn't signaling you from the bow of the ship, Saegar. How could I? I didn't even believe that mermaids—not to mention mermen—really existed. All I was doing when I bowed was trying not to vomit from seasickness. And as for calling you in 'sealenese'—or whatever seal language is called—well, I wasn't doing that, either. I was gagging."

Saegar lifted his eyebrows skeptically, but said, "Fine. If this is so, release me and prove your innocence."

"But—"

"Make no more excuses, Beth Living Stone," he interrupted coldly. "Who captured me or why is no longer of importance. It is my release that concerns me now."

He drew himself up proudly until he was waist deep in the water, and once again folded his arms over his broad, tanned chest. His voice held a distinctly commanding note as he declared, "I now claim a boon—a reward—for sparing the life of your Ralph."

"He's not my Ralph!" Beth protested. "But never mind," she added hastily, as Saegar's brows lowered over his eyes again. "Please. Go on."

He eyed her warningly for a moment, then—as she remained silent—continued in an imperious tone, "In return for the life of Ralph, I demand that you help me escape tonight in the hours before dawn. So that I may return to Pacifica, to find my sisters and aid my people."

His gaze locked with hers. Determination was etched in every line of his face as he waited—as stiff and unyielding as a bronzed statue—for her to respond.

His regal attitude was contagious. The lofty yet compelling demand in his voice, in his eyes, made her feel so—so solemn. Like she was in church. Or maybe in court, about to swear an oath before a judge.

Beth swallowed to ease the dryness in her throat. She straightened her own back and returned his steady stare, her expression becoming as grave as his.

"I will release you, Saegar, to return to your home in Pacifica, so that you can aid your people," she said, unconsciously mimicking the formal phrases and cadence he had used. "On my word of honor, I promise to do this...."

His eyes blazed with triumph.

Beth bit her lip. "But...just not tonight."

Chapter Seven

His eyes flared again—this time with rage. Beth jumped as he slapped the water violently with his hand. "You mock—you *toy* with me, Beth Living Stone!"

"I'm not mocking! And I never toy—"

"*Tonight* you will release me," he demanded between clenched teeth. "In the hours just before dawn, when the rest of the ship sleeps."

"I want to, but I can't. Not tonight. I told you my father's taken a turn for the worse. The shock of learning that you're gone—well, I'm almost certain it would kill him." Beth spread her hands in a helpless gesture, trying to make him understand. "I need—*he* needs a little time to get stronger again before I give him news like that. A couple of days until he's out of danger. Then I'll help you escape."

"Nay!"

"Saegar, we have no choice."

His mouth twisted bitterly. "In truth, what you mean is that I have no choice."

"Neither do I," she insisted. "I can't jeopardize my father's life when a short delay would hurt no one. You're already ten years late, Saegar. Do a few more days really make any difference?"

"Every second makes a difference when you are being held a prisoner."

She couldn't argue with that, so she didn't even try. Instead, she said softly, "Please, Saegar. I know I have no right to ask, but please, can you give me just two more days? We'll probably need the time anyway to figure out how we're going to do this—"

She broke off as he suddenly held up his hand again in that imperative demand for silence. Tilting his head, he glanced toward the stairs. Beth looked in that direction, too, and a second later, saw the door open at the top of the staircase.

"Ralph!" she breathed in surprise, as her father's assistant stepped through the door. "What is he doing here?"

She glanced at Saegar as she spoke, but he didn't respond, merely regarded her with a sardonic expression as he retreated into the shadows beneath the platform.

Something in his eyes made her feel self-conscious. She looked toward the staircase again, watching Ralph walk carefully across the small landing, his hand pressed against his cracked ribs.

"Elizabeth?" he called, leaning over the railing to peer down at her. "Apple dumpling, what are you doing down there so late?" He frowned, as he saw her bedraggled appearance. "You're all wet."

"I'm checking on the merman. He just...splashed me a little," she answered, restraining a wince at the 'apple dumpling' endearment. "Why are you here? I thought you weren't supposed to leave your bed."

"I'm not. I've probably set back my recovery by a week or more. But I waited over an hour for you to join me for dinner and I began to get worried. Delano told me you took one of my specimens down there, and I thought I'd better come see what's going on."

"Nothing's going on, Ralph," she assured him, refusing to feel guilty despite the reproach in his tone. He could have sent Dougie to check on her, after all, instead of coming himself.

"Although…" She paused, then decided she might as well get her confession over with immediately. "Although the merman did eat your prize piranha. I'd brought it down to keep him company."

"Oh, my God…" Ralph clapped a hand to his forehead, then lowered it with a sigh. "When will you learn, Beth? He's not human." He glanced over to where Saegar still lingered in the shadows, and his voice hardened. "You have to quit trying to treat him like one."

Beth glanced at Saegar, too, and raised her eyebrows slightly, hoping Ralph's remark would prompt him to change his mind and speak up after all. But he simply returned her gaze expressionlessly.

Suppressing a sigh, she called up to Ralph, "Yes, well, I'm sorry about your fish."

He waved his hand in a dismissive gesture. "Never mind that now. Just come to dinner."

"I'll be right there after I change."

Ralph nodded. After a final glare in Saegar's direction, he left, the door swinging shut behind him.

Beth glanced at Saegar, too. "I have to go," she said, feeling awkward for some reason. "If I don't, he'll probably come back and he might catch us talking next time. You're sure you don't want me to tell him—"

"Tell him nothing."

She sighed. "All right. It's your decision." She hesitated, and then added, "So are we okay?"

"Okay?"

"I mean, do you understand why I need a few more days?"

"I understand that you give me no choice," Saegar answered, anger edging his tone. "If this is another trick, Beth Living Stone…"

"It's not. You can count on me." She held up her hand like a Girl Scout taking a pledge. "I promise."

He stared at her with narrowed eyes. "So we will see."

Saegar assumed he had told Beth Living Stone enough to satisfy her. He discovered his mistake the next morning. The night darkness ringed by the porthole had barely lightened to a hazy gray when the little female came trotting down the stairs to sit on the platform and pelt him with more questions.

She'd donned a white shirt and blue breeches hugged the curves of her hips. Her feet were encased in brown leather sandals. A silver ring twinkled on one of her small toes, and she'd painted her nails the soft glowing pink of a summer sunset.

This morning her changeable eyes were a dark blue, Saegar noticed, like the fish that darted among the coral near the Florida coast, and—like the little fish—full of curiosity. He floated in the middle of the tank, rubbing his sore shoulder to relieve the stiffness there as he tried to answer her questions about his home.

"Pacifica is a series of caves, joined by canals," he told her almost brusquely, growing tired of trying to explain.

Beth gave a little shudder. "It sounds a bit grim. Are

they damp? Moldy? Are you sure you can't be more specific?"

"Nay."

"Please, Saegar. I just want to know. What is Pacifica really like?"

"Like home." Already the air in the hold felt humid. He ducked beneath the surface to cool off, and arose to her next question.

"What do you mean it's like home?" Beth demanded, before he could disappear beneath the water again.

He shrugged, his wet, brown shoulders gleaming with the lazy movement. "Full of light. Warmth."

"Light?" She raised her eyebrows. "So you have electricity, like we do?" She glanced at the lights lining the walls.

Saegar glanced at them, too. "Nay. The lights of Pacifica are softer, yet more brilliant. Like the phosphorous on the waves."

Beth frowned. "No electricity? That sounds a little primitive."

He stiffened. "Primitive?"

"More basic, I mean," she corrected herself hastily. "Is it a big place?"

Saegar thought about that as he began to rotate his arm, grunting a little at the pulling sensation on his wound the movement caused. "Nay."

"Small? Like the size of this ship?"

"Nay. Bigger."

She heaved an exasperated sigh. "Well, that sure paints a vivid picture."

Reluctant amusement tugged at his mouth at the disgruntlement in her voice. The little female's curiosity was boundless, he decided, and her arrogance as well. Obviously, she imagined Pacifica to be an uncivilized, unsophisticated place compared with her own country. "Why do you need to know all these things?"

She leaned back on her hands, her hair spilling down over her shoulders. The gold in the silky strands glinted in the dim morning light as she tilted her head to consider the question. He imagined how it would glisten floating free beneath the waves.

"I ask so that I can get to know you better, I suppose," she said. "To help me understand what your people are like."

"You believe you can know an entire people, by talking with just one?"

"No, of course not," Beth conceded. "But it's a start."

Saegar studied her. The sincerity in her eyes, in her earnest voice, eased his resentment at her continual questioning. Yet he was still unsure how to describe the home he'd left so long ago.

He had been but six when he had last seen Pacifica. And he remembered his homeland, in truth he did. But his memories were those of the heart. He recalled the tenderness in his mother's smile, the feel of his father's big hand squeezing his shoulder proudly. The adoring gazes of his baby sisters, Phoebe and Kai, and the grief on eight-year-old Thalassa's pretty face, when they'd said goodbye.

Yet, even those remembrances had softened, grown misty with the passage of time. After twenty-five years in exile, memories of love had become entangled with loss, until they were almost as painful to remember as they were to forget.

Much easier to talk about were his years at sea. Many days—months—had simply drifted past in lonely boredom, but these he did not mention. Instead he told Beth

Living Stone about the dangers he'd faced—the monstrous storms, the deadly sea predators—pleased when her blue-green eyes grew big and round with wonder at his first tale, and bigger yet at his second.

"...So I twisted and dived, and the massive jaws of the great white shark closed mere inches from my arm. I turned, and with the quickness of a striking eel, I plunged my knife into his thick hide again—and again—until the sea glowed red from his blood, and at last, the giant was dead." Saegar concluded his third tale with a dramatic, highly satisfactory jab of his imaginary knife into the air. He held the pose a moment—arm braced, biceps bulging—before letting his hand fall. Then he glanced at Beth, awaiting her praise.

She was now sitting with her legs crossed, her elbow resting on her knee, her chin propped in her palm. Only this time, instead of being wide with wonder as they had been after his previous stories, her eyes were narrowed as she studied him thoughtfully. "Goodness. I'm surprised there are any sharks left, it sounds like you've vanquished so many."

He lifted a brow. "Do you doubt my prowess with a knife, Beth Living Stone?"

"Not at all," she responded politely. "I was just wondering where your knife was when Ralph cap—picked you up."

His expression closed. "I lost it. The day Bali died."

He hadn't even realized it was gone at first, that he'd dropped it when he saw the old man lying in the surf. He'd rushed to his friend, and held his frail frame in his arms, listening as Bali bid him to return home to Pacifica. When Bali breathed no more, Saegar had started out without bothering to recover his weapon, grief at the loss of his mentor mingling with the joy of knowing that his long exile had ended at last.

Only to blunder like a blind seal into Ralph's net.

A frown crossed his face, and his tail twitched angrily. He slanted a considering look at the little female's face. "I have need of a knife, Beth Living Stone."

Her eyes widened, and she shook her head. "No, you don't. There are no sharks around here."

"Nay, not for sharks," he said, giving her a reproachful look. A tangle of damp hair fell over his forehead. Slicking it back with a careless hand, he told her, "My hair annoys me. I need a knife to cut it shorter."

"Well, I don't have a knife—and I wouldn't give it to you if I did," Beth said, not mincing matters. "You might get hurt if you try to cut your hair yourself with that sore shoulder, so I'll do it for you. Not with a knife," she assured him, in response to his frown. "But with scissors."

He studied her expression a moment and his frown deepened. He shook his head. "Nay, it is not important."

"But I don't mind—"

"Nay, it is not important, Beth Living Stone," he interrupted her abruptly. "And I grow weary of talking. I must swim to keep up my strength or even the terrapin will pass me in the ocean on my way home."

"You look pretty strong to me," Beth murmured, but he'd already dived beneath the surface, to begin his endless laps.

Nor did he stop again for the next few hours. Beth went to sit by her sleeping father for a while to give Anne a short break, and when she returned to the hold, Saegar was still swimming. He stopped, however, when she began to spread his lunch out on the cloth she'd

HOW TO PLAY:

1. With a coin, carefully scratch off the 3 gold areas on your Lucky Carnival Wheel. By doing so you have qualified to receive everything revealed—2 FREE books and a surprise gift—ABSOLUTELY FREE!

2. Send back this card and you'll receive 2 brand-new Silhouette Romance® novels. These books have a cover price of $3.99 each in the U.S. and $4.50 each in Canada, but they are yours ABSOLUTELY FREE.

3. There's no catch! You're under no obligation to buy anything. We charge nothing—ZERO—for your first shipment. And you don't have to make any minimum number of purchases—not even one!

4. The fact is thousands of readers enjoy receiving books by mail from the Silhouette Reader Service™. They enjoy the convenience of home delivery...they like getting the best new novels at discount prices, BEFORE they're available in stores... and they love their *Heart to Heart* subscriber newsletter featuring author news, horoscopes, recipes, book reviews and much more!

5. We hope that after receiving your free books you'll want to remain a subscriber. But the choice is yours—to continue or cancel, any time at all! So why not take us up on our invitation, with no risk of any kind. You'll be glad you did!

A surprise gift
FREE
We can't tell you what it is...but we're sure you'll like it! A
FREE GIFT!
just for playing LUCKY CARNIVAL WHEEL!

Visit us online at
www.eHarlequin.com

LUCKY **Carnival Wheel**
Find Out Instantly The Gifts You Get **Absolutely FREE!**
Scratch-off Game

Scratch off **ALL 3** Gold areas

YES! I have scratched off the 3 Gold Areas above.
Please send me the 2 FREE books and gift for
which I qualify! I understand I am under no obligation to purchase
any books, as explained on the back and on the opposite page.

315 SDL DNW9   215 SDL DNW3

FIRST NAME	LAST NAME

ADDRESS

APT.#	CITY

STATE/PROV.	ZIP/POSTAL CODE

The Silhouette Reader Service™—Here's how it works:

Accepting your 2 free books and gift places you under no obligation to buy anything. You may keep the books and gift and return the shipping statement marked "cancel." If you do not cancel, about a month later we'll send you 6 additional novels and bill you just $3.34 each in the U.S., or $3.80 each in Canada, plus 25¢ shipping & handling per book and applicable taxes if any.* That's the complete price and — compared to cover prices of $3.99 each in the U.S. and $4.50 each in Canada—it's quite a bargain! You may cancel at any time, but if you choose to continue, every month we'll send you 6 more books, which you may either purchase at the discount price or return to us and cancel your subscription.

*Terms and prices subject to change without notice. Sales tax applicable in N.Y. Canadian residents will be charged applicable provincial taxes and GST.

If offer card is missing write to: Silhouette Reader Service, 3010 Walden Ave., P.O. Box 1867, Buffalo, NY 14240-1867

BUSINESS REPLY MAIL

FIRST-CLASS MAIL   PERMIT NO. 717-003   BUFFALO, NY

POSTAGE WILL BE PAID BY ADDRESSEE

SILHOUETTE READER SERVICE
3010 WALDEN AVE
PO BOX 1867
BUFFALO NY 14240-9952

NO POSTAGE
NECESSARY
IF MAILED
IN THE
UNITED STATES

brought, to hoist himself as he usually did, his chest resting on the platform, his lower body still in the water. Saegar surveyed her offering, then his dark brows drew down into a scowl. "No more fish eggs?"

"You ate it all. Have some spinach." She shoved it over to him. "Popeye's favorite."

"Pop eye?" His curiosity piqued, Saegar raised a questioning eyebrow. "A blowfish?"

"A sailor man—but never mind that," she added hastily, when he appeared about to pursue the subject. "Tell me more about Bali, and this cove he took you to. Was it special somehow? Why did you stay there?"

Saegar shrugged. Ripping off a piece of the lettuce of Pop Eye, he chewed and swallowed. "Bali was old—he preferred the warmer waters of the south as well as the isolation. The seas are not as vast as they once were, with your huge warships and pleasure boats crowding the waves and he would take no chances at being seen. Bali hated your kind," Saegar said bluntly, taking another bite of lettuce. "The pollution your people cause, the butchering of the whales—"

"I hate those things too!" Beth protested, stung by the condemnation in his voice. "And many of 'my kind' as you call them, are trying to correct such atrocities. Although, it's much easier, I'm sure, to simply hide out to avoid all those evils."

"I did not hide out," Saegar responded, his jaw tightening. "Unlike Bali, I was young—and foolish," he added, with a grim twist of his mouth. "I was unwilling to trade my freedom for safety. From the age of sixteen or so, I traveled off on my own for most of the year to explore the colder waters of the Atlantic, up to the Arctic seas, so rich with sea life."

He paused, chewing his spinach, his expression brooding as he remembered. "I wanted to see the world for myself—not just be told of it, through an old man's tales," he admitted finally. "I also wanted to learn about your people for myself. So I did."

"How?" Beth asked.

He shrugged, and picked up a piece of halibut. "I would linger near boats at night, or beneath docks during the day. And I would listen."

"Are our people so different from yours? Is our society?" Beth asked, wondering if maybe the relationships of his people were…looser than those of hers. "Do you have marriage on Pacifica?"

The question annoyed Saegar. Certainly they had marriage on Pacifica—although *wedlock* was the term more commonly used. Yet, if once again Beth Living Stone was so quick to believe his homeland had to be more primitive than hers, his people more barbaric, then who was he to tell her different?

He shrugged. "We mate—just as you do."

The color rising in her cheeks pleased him. "I don't— I mean, marriage doesn't mean mating exactly," she said, then frowned as she thought that over. "Well, in a way it does," she admitted reluctantly. "But it's more than that."

He lifted a brow. "How so?"

"Marriage is the legal ceremony showing that two people love each other."

"So this marriage only happens for love?"

"Yes…well, no. That's the idea, but unfortunately, people often get married for all kinds of reasons. Some marry for money, some because they want children. Some people even marry just so they can stay in the country."

Seeing his frown deepen at that, she explained, "Not

everyone is allowed to just come and stay in my country, Saegar. You either have to be born there, apply for citizenship, or marry someone who is already a citizen. That's called a Green Card marriage. And usually when people marry, a woman takes the man's last name and adds it to her own. That way when their children are born, everyone knows which family they belong to. Who their father is. Don't they have surnames on Pacifica?''

Saegar curled his lip. ''On Pacifica, everyone knows who their father is. And their family as well.''

''They know in my world, too—usually,'' Beth said defensively. ''So all Pacificans only have one name?''

''Nay, we have several,'' Saegar declared, not to be outdone by the dirt dwellers. ''At birth, we are given a name that has meaning—not like this surname you refer to. I am Saegar which means Sea Warrior or Sea Spear—''

''How Freud would love that,'' Beth murmured.

Saegar's eyes narrowed. ''Who is this Freud you speak of?''

''Never mind,'' Beth said, waving her hand dismissingly. ''You were saying? About names?''

He eyed her suspiciously for a moment longer, then continued, ''Aye, Pacificans bear names of honor and pride, given in recognition of our deeds. I am known as Saegar the Brave, Saegar the Strong and—'' his teeth flashed in a sharkish grin ''—Saegar the Lusty.''

He should add Saegar the Conceited to that list, Beth decided silently.

''We do not need a ceremony to give us names,'' he added. ''Nor would a female of Pacifica bind herself to a man she did not love, simply to please her father.''

Beth stiffened. ''I don't understand what you're talking about.''

"Do you not?" he asked, mockery in his voice.

Their gazes locked, then she quickly looked away and rose to her feet. "I've got to go. I promised to stop by to see Ralph this afternoon before dinner."

"And do you always keep your promises, Beth Living Stone?"

"Yes," she replied firmly as she turned away. "I do."

Chapter Eight

Beth loitered at the bottom of the staircase when she returned that evening, reluctant to face any more of Saegar's sardonic questions about marriage. He'd caught her off guard earlier, with his oblique references to her father's hopes for her and Ralph. If only she hadn't said all those things when she'd thought he couldn't understand. She cast an annoyed look at the tank, and discovered Saegar had halted in his swimming, and was watching her over the top.

"You are late with the meal, Beth Living Stone," he said as their eyes met.

It wasn't a reproof, just a statement of fact, but Beth stiffened defensively. She watched as he pushed away from the side of the tank to head toward the platform. When he reached it, he turned and with his back to the structure, grasped the edge and slowly raised himself out of the water, rubbing his shoulder along the wood. He repeated the strange backwards pull-up again. Then again.

"What are you doing?" Beth demanded.

"My wound," he told her without pausing. "It annoys me."

With a sigh of exasperation, Beth crossed the floor to the platform. "You're going to make it bleed again if you keep doing that," she said, as she climbed the steps. She walked out onto the middle of the structure to scowl at the top of his head. "Saegar, don't!"

He paused in midlift, his arm muscles bulging to frown up at her. "It itches."

"Well, don't do that anyway. You'll hurt yourself. I'll get some ointment from Anne and rub it on for you," she promised. "That will make you feel better."

He gave her an odd look. "Nay, it would not."

Releasing the wood, he slid into the water. He sank beneath the surface, then rose again, his tanned skin gleaming wetly.

He raised his torso up on the platform as usual to eat, waiting patiently while she removed his dinner from the bag she'd brought, while his lower body remained in the water.

"So, Beth Living Stone," he said, as he picked up a piece of the smoked salmon she'd brought him. "Did you keep your promise? Did you visit your Ralph?"

"He's not my—" Beth bit back the denial, her lips tightening. "Yes."

Saegar lifted a brow at her clipped reply. "So is he no longer ill?"

"He's fine. Almost," she added grudgingly.

"Ah, then perhaps he might decide to pay me another visit, before I leave tomorrow night." He smiled, then ripped off another piece of the fish with his strong white teeth.

He didn't say anything more as he continued eating,

and neither did Beth. But when he finished and before he could drop back off the platform, she said casually, "Speaking of promises..." and pulled out the scissors she'd tucked in the bag with his food.

She held them up. "So what about it? Ready for a haircut?" She clicked the scissors invitingly, and gave him a reassuring smile. "C'mon, Saegar. I won't hurt you. I promise. You don't need to be afraid."

Saegar had allowed his gaze to drop to Beth Living Stone's mouth, but at her last remark his eyes jerked up to meet hers, his back stiffening. He frowned at her. She gave him an innocent look—which darkened his scowl even more.

He felt uneasy at her offer of so personal a service. He did not want the little female to come close; to stir up that restless mixture of urgency and desire hidden inside him. But afraid of her puny shears? Nay, never!

"Cut it," he said curtly.

She immediately came over, and knelt by his side. Saegar tensed slightly, and looked straight ahead as she leaned closer—close enough that he could feel her warmth.

She speared her fingers lightly through his damp hair, stroking his scalp. A tingle spread along his skin. His pulse quickened, but Saegar kept his expression blank.

"Hmm." She lifted a strand. "Pretty healthy looking, considering that it's constantly doused in saltwater. Do you want it short or—"

"Short."

"Short it is then."

Beth began working, gently pushing his head this way and that to get a better angle as she cut, amazed at how thick and glossy his hair was. The dark, rich brown reminded her of polished walnut. Saegar had fallen silent and when she glanced at his face, she saw that his gaze was preoccupied as he stared along the platform.

He was obviously content to remain silent, but Beth wanted to talk—to find out something.

Gently tilting his head a bit more to the side, she snipped off another length of hair then said, "Saegar..."

He gave an absent grunt.

"I was wondering. Did other mer people visit you and Bali at the cove?"

"Nay. The cove is a place known only to my family. I only saw my fellow mer during my travels. And not many at that."

"Oh." She clipped around his ear. "Just mermen?"

"Maids also."

"I see." She clipped some more, allowing a few seconds to pass before adding casually, "Did they stay with you long?"

"Nay...except Mariah. A maid I met at sixteen."

"Mariah," Beth said flatly. "That's a pretty name."

"Aye," Saegar agreed, considering the matter. To the mer, her name meant "As the Wind"—and it suited her. Like the wind she'd been; always on the move.

She'd been his first lover, but though he'd been young, he'd known better than to become attached. Mariah's parents had fled Pacifica with her about the same time he'd been exiled. She'd been raised among humans, traveling from one country to another. Possibly as a result, Mariah's nature had been too restless to allow her to remain in one place—or with one man—for too long. Still, she had been a beautiful female, there was no denying that. He added reminiscently, "She was a magnificent siren, with midnight eyes and hair."

Beth's lips tightened at his reply. She lifted another hank of hair, tugging hard enough to make Saegar give her a sideways glance. "Sorry," she said. She cut the hair off a trifle viciously. "What happened to her?"

Saegar shrugged. "She was on her way to see Pacifica, which she had not seen since she was a child. Because my exile had not yet ended, we parted."

He fell silent again, and Beth did, too, wishing she'd never brought the subject up. The whole thing was oddly depressing. She'd felt...irritated, hearing him talk about Mariah, but she felt sorry for him, too, upon learning how his banishment had affected even that area of his life.

Still, there was nothing she could do, so she forced herself to put Mariah—and Saegar's story—from her mind. Cutting his hair was the only thing she could do to help him at the moment, so she concentrated on the task, becoming absorbed in doing the best job possible.

Saegar remained silent, too. He thought about Mariah a short time, then about Pacifica, but neither could hold his attention. Mariah, long forgotten until today, was in his past; his return to Pacifica, yet in the future. All he could focus on was the present...and Beth Living Stone.

He tried not to tense as she shifted around him, to keep his expression blank. Yet it grew harder and harder to hide his reaction at her nearness. At times her encircling arms almost brushed his face she was so close. Her skin was damp from the heat, and smelled pleasant—like the yellow flowers that grew along the shores of the Caribbean Islands. When he shivered, tickled by the hair falling on his bare shoulders and chest, she laughed—a liquid feminine sound—and brushed the strands away. Her touch was impersonal, yet the feel of her soft fingertips seemed to linger on his skin.

His blood heated and thickened in his veins. Lowering his lashes to shield his gaze, Saegar watched her face.

Her expression was intent. A small frown furrowed her brow, and she'd pursed her red lips together. The way she tilted her own head back and forth in conjunction with his, the faint unconscious hums of approval she made as she worked, made his lips curve in a faint smile. Then she leaned closer as she reached to cut his hair in the back and Saegar's smile disappeared. His pulse beat harder, faster. She was wearing a short, sky-blue sheath, sleeveless and cut low above her breasts. The simple lines of the garment showed off her lovely neck and revealed her delicately hollowed collarbones, inviting exploring kisses. Her breasts—mere inches from his face—swelled against the thin material in soft, alluring curves.

"All done," Beth said. She briskly brushed the remaining bits of hair off his shoulders, and sat back on her heels to survey her handiwork. "Not bad if I do say so myself. Short, but with the tousled, windblown look that's in style right now with the Brad Pitt wanna-bes— and I imagine in style also for mermen at sea."

He didn't reply, and she glanced at his face. "Saegar?" Was he...yes, he was! He was staring at her breasts with an intent, almost hungry look, his eyes half-closed, his lips faintly parted.

Her eyes widened, her grip tightened on the scissors. In response to his expression sudden heat raced over Beth's skin, quickly followed by a dew of perspiration. She shivered as the moisture cooled her flesh, and her nipples peaked sharply. She could actually feel them pressing against her cotton top, as if welcoming his avid gaze.

Instinctively, she lifted her hands to cover them and his hands snaked out, catching her wrists to stop the movement. His lean, strong fingers shackled her wrists.

Slowly, he spread her arms out to the side, looking his fill.

Her breath caught on a small gasp. Beneath his dark tan, a faint red stained his high cheekbones. His lashes lifted, his gaze meeting hers. Beth shivered again at the smoldering heat in his dark-blue eyes.

Then his gaze dropped to her mouth. Was he going to kiss her?

"Saegar?" she said uncertainly.

His grip tightened...then he released her. Avoiding her gaze, he eased away, lowering himself back down into the water.

Beth rose shakily to her feet, trying to decide what to do—and quickly reached the conclusion that the only thing to do was to pretend nothing had happened. Striving to appear nonchalant, she gathered up the remaining bits of hair she'd cut and tossed them in the bag along with the scissors.

"Well, okay. That's...done," she said in a bright voice, without looking in his direction. And she made her escape.

Outside, she paused, leaned against the railing while she waited for her pulse to settle. Despite the cool breeze caressing her cheeks, she felt hot and flushed.

Nothing happened, she assured herself. Not really. Just a bit of—of hormonal upheaval. And she knew what had caused it. All that talk, her questions about Mariah had obviously gotten Saegar's libido stirred up. Probably any halfway decent female would appear attractive after months—possibly years—of forced abstinence.

Even a human female.

She looked down at her legs, then lifted her skirt a few inches higher on her thighs. They weren't bad—slender and fairly long. Decent knees and ankles. And her feet were small, with toes that lined up in a neatly descending line. Still, to Saegar, a human's legs were probably hideous, Beth realized, her toes curling at the thought. After all, hadn't she thought he'd looked strange when she'd first seen his tail?

But the odd thing was, she barely noticed their differences anymore when she looked at him. All she could see was the strength in his face, the intelligence in his eyes, the wry humor that so often twisted his mouth, his—

Whoa, this line of thinking needs to stop right now! Beth told herself. She couldn't be getting a—a crush on a man that was half fish! She was being ridiculous to even think about such a thing. Talk about a mismatch!

Still, it was a good thing he was leaving tomorrow. She might feel sad for a while—okay, she'd feel rotten— but at least she could get off this emotional roller coaster she'd somehow climbed onto before things got completely out of hand.

But even that reassurance faded rapidly when she reached her father's door. Anne answered her knock, and stepped outside to talk to her privately, telling her that Carl shouldn't be disturbed.

"Dad's even worse?" Beth said, getting right to the pertinent point of the news Anne was couching in medical terms.

"Not worse. He's just not better yet," Anne insisted. "He's not young anymore, Beth. He just needs a little longer to recover from this virus and then you'll be able to visit him, I promise. Two more days isn't that long to wait, is it?"

"No, of course not," Beth agreed with a sigh. No, two more days didn't matter that much. And surely Saegar would see it that way, too.

Chapter Nine

Saegar was awake early the next morning—his last aboard *The Searcher*. And though he'd gotten but little sleep the night before, he felt well prepared for his escape that night. His wound was almost healed, and he felt full of restless energy. Able to swim one hundred leagues before the next dawn if need be—nay, two— mayhap three hundred!

Getting off the ship would be difficult, of course. The body that served him so well in the water was a burden on land. But he had faith in the strength of his upper body, to compensate for the lack of legs. All he needed was for Beth to release that cursed lock on the door, then serve as lookout, in case anyone should espy them.

Aye, he would do it, with the little female's help. He glanced over at her as she sat on the platform. Sunlight poured down through the porthole above her like bright, liquid gold, hitting the water with a sparkle before bouncing gaily against the drab walls of the hold. A shaft of light spilled over Beth Living Stone as well, flickering over her silky brown hair, yellow shirt and tan shorts.

She looked deceptively slight, vulnerable almost as she sat there in her usual pose, her bare arms wrapped around her legs with her small chin resting on her knees. She'd been oddly silent all morning, and was now contemplating her toes, as if they held the answers to all the problems in the universe.

She looked pensive, distracted, and a spark of irritation ignited inside him. He'd grown accustomed to having her full attention. To seeing the bright interest in her eyes as she watched him, of basking in the warmth of her winsome smile. Was she acting so withdrawn because he'd wanted to touch her yesterday? His jaw tightened at the thought, then he discarded it. She was not acting self-conscious or angry. Merely preoccupied, as if she had something else on her mind.

Or maybe *someone* else. Could she be thinking of Ralph? he wondered. The man her father wished her to marry?

His annoyance grew stronger. Surely not. This was their last day together; she should not be lost in some daydream about another man. She should be paying attention to him!

He scooped up a handful of water and tossed it at her. Startled, she glanced up, then frowned at him as she brushed the glistening drops from her bare legs. "You're always getting me wet!" she said—then added hurriedly, "With water, I mean."

Saegar stared at her, intrigued by the pink flush flooding her cheeks, the embarrassment in her expression. "What other way is there?"

"Never mind," Beth murmured. "It's not important."

After a few seconds, she looked down at her feet again, the brooding look returning to her face.

His brows drew down in annoyance. "Talk to me," he demanded.

"Hmm?" Beth glanced at him, then realized what he'd said. She raised her eyebrows. "I thought you were tired of hearing my busy tongue."

"Aye, but silence on your part is not normal."

She smiled a little. "Yes, it is. Usually I'm not so chatty as I've been with you."

He arched an eyebrow. "This I find hard to believe, Beth Living Stone. And it does not explain why you are so subdued."

"I'm not subdued, I'm just…" She glanced away from him, and shifted restlessly, glancing up at the porthole overhead. "Hot. It's so hot today. I wish there was some way to shade that."

She slipped off her sandals, and scooted over to sit at the edge of the platform, and dangle her feet in the water. She looked down, idly kicking at the water as she said, "Saegar…"

"Aye?"

"Do you ever wish you were not meremer? That you had legs, like the mer do?"

"Wishing is for children, Beth Living Stone. I am…as I am. This tail that makes me so different, so primitive to your untutored eyes, will take me where I need to go. Home to Pacifica."

Before she could move her feet away, he caught hold of her ankle, wrapping his fingers around it to keep her in place. Beth tensed, and he glanced at her mockingly. "I wish to examine these legs you think so superior to my fins. A little thin, I think. Rather puny and weak for swimming, but not bad for walking, I suppose. And so smooth.'' He ran his finger caressingly up from her ankle, along the curve of her calf to her knee. ''So white…''

Beth's skin tingled at his touch and her cheeks flushed with pleasure.

''Like the underbelly of a cod,'' he added blandly, watching her expression.

She stiffened. ''Why you—'' She tried to kick free of his grip. ''Well, that's a compliment to treasure. Even less appealing than Ralph's usual ones.''

His grasp tightened. ''Ah, Ralph.''

Something in his voice made Beth's insides quiver. She glanced down at him, but Saegar had lowered his chin and nose into the water until only his narrowed eyes remained above the surface. Like an alligator, she thought. Eyeing its prey.

Raising his head from the water, he asked silkily, ''Is he your lover?''

''What? No!''

''But he desires to be.''

She remained stubbornly silent. His narrowed gaze studied her face, but when it became apparent she wasn't going to answer, his gaze drifted down, settling on her legs again.

His brows drew together in a frown. ''What are these?'' he demanded, gently touching the marks on her knees.

Beth looked down at her legs, too, to see what he was talking about. His big hand looked so dark against her skin. His fingers were long, encircling her ankle with ease. She tried to ignore them, concentrating on the faint bruises on her knees. ''I fell when I was climbing the stairs awhile back.''

His frown disappeared, replaced by a sardonic expression. "Ah, yes. I remember. The day you saw my tail. You scampered up the stairs like a clumsy sea otter scaling a cliff."

"I did not!"

"Aye, you did. And like a curious little otter, you could not resist sliding back down again. Back to me." His grasp on her ankle tightened. "So come in and play, Beth Living Stone."

Beth didn't know how it happened. One second she was sitting sedately on the platform, the next she was in the cold, salty water. Bubbles whirled around her, water rushed into her eyes, her mouth. She reached out blindly, and her hand struck a hard muscular chest. Saegar.

She clutched at him and his strong arm locked around her waist. She threw her arms around the sturdy column of his neck, holding on with all her might. His arms tightened around her, then with effortless ease, Saegar hauled her to the surface again.

He held her there, cradled against his hard chest, his teeth flashing in a smile at her bewildered expression and the water streaming down her face. Then he shifted his grip to clasp her around the waist. Lifting his arms, he lightly tossed her back up to where she'd been sitting.

Beth rolled onto her back, staring up at the beams overhead as she coughed and sputtered. Saegar raised himself up on the platform, leaning on his crossed arms as he watched her.

"You certainly do not swim like an otter," he pointed out. "You must learn to keep your mouth shut, Beth Living Stone, when you swim underwater."

"I can't swim at all," Beth managed to gasp out.

"No kidding," he said solemnly, repeating a phrase he'd heard her use often—then chuckled aloud at the surprised expression on her face.

Beth pushed back the wet hair clinging to her cheeks, and shakily sat up to stare at him. She hadn't heard him laugh before, she realized. The amusement in his eyes, the teasing smile on his mouth, changed his hard visage completely. He looked younger, carefree—the way he probably would have looked if he'd never left Pacifica. The way he would look when he was free of the ship— and her—and he reached home once again.

Her heart clenched. And that would be soon. Oh, not tonight, as he thought, but still soon enough.

Her eyes burned. From the salt in the tank, she assured herself stoutly, as she brushed the wetness from her lashes.

She saw that Saegar was watching her, the amusement on his face fading to a somber expression. "Did I hurt you, little one?"

"No, of course not." For some reason, the unusual gentleness in his tone made a lump swell in her throat. Beth swallowed, forcing it away, but her voice still sounded husky as she added, "It's just—well, there's something I need to talk to you about. There's been a slight change in plans." She glanced away, and rose shakily to her feet. Gathering up the bottom of her shirt, she began wringing it out in an effort to avoid his gaze.

Staring at her averted face, Saegar felt something tighten inside him. "What change?" he demanded.

Beth drew a deep breath, and let go of her shirt. She met his gaze fleetingly, then quickly looked away again, brushing the water from her arms and legs. "My father is still sick. We need to wait a few more days before I can help you make your escape."

"No."

His implacable tone brought her gaze up. And when

Beth looked at his face, she saw that his expression was implacable as well.

She spread her hands in a helpless gesture. "I'm sorry, Saegar, but he hasn't gotten better. In the condition he's still in, it could kill him if he knew I released you."

"Do not tell him."

"He'd find out anyway, from Ralph or the Delanos."

He didn't reply to that, so she added persuasively, "It's just a small delay—"

"No!" He cut her off, slashing the air with his hand. "I am not a slave to be held against my will any longer," he told her grimly, his eyes cold, his mouth pressed into a thin line.

"I know. I want to let you go tonight. I just can't."

His eyes flashed, then his lids half-closed. His deep voice assumed a bored tone that failed to hide the lash of anger behind it. "Nay, of course you cannot. If you did, who would you have to talk to? To play with and caress? You would lose your pet."

She stiffened. "I don't treat you like that!"

"Do you not, Beth Living Stone?"

"No!"

"I say you are a liar as well as a coward. So afraid of losing your father's love, that you will do anything to please him—even make my life a misery, display me as a freak to be marveled and gawked at. Make your own a misery too, by mating with a man that you do not love."

She whitened. "That's not true. I just don't want him to be hurt."

The expression on Saegar's face was utterly cold, utterly contemptuous. "Lie to yourself, if you please. But do not come down into this hellhole again to lie to me."

* * *

She left.

The lock spun, then caught with a taunting click. Saegar waited—long, endless minutes. The door did not reopen.

Finally, he turned away from the stairs. He made his way toward the platform, swimming slowly, the water whispering and murmuring around him with soft sighs of regret.

In his mind, he heard Bali's voice as well, creaky and rusty as an old battleship riding the waves. *They are land dwellers, Saegar, and not of our kind. Never let them come close. They are not to be trusted.*

Flattening his palms against the warm wood, Saegar hoisted himself up on the platform, lifting his entire body clear of the water. He fell lengthwise along the planks, landing on his back in the damp patch where she'd lain.

The harsh light from the porthole overhead made him squint. He threw up his arm, shading his eyes from the glare. The hot sun, magnified by the thick glass, poured down over him. It seared his skin—his scales. But he endured the pain, lying still.

He had no choice. He had trusted her…and she'd lied. He would not make the same mistake again. He needed to escape tonight, before the ship drew any closer to San Diego, no matter what the cost.

Time passed. His mouth grew dry, his lips parched and cracked. Along his body the burning pain increased. Yet inside he felt cold, as the warm thoughts of home that had sustained him for so long melted away, replaced by a new, icy purpose.

To make her pay, for all he'd lost.

Chapter Ten

For the rest of the day and well into the night, Beth wrestled with her conscience. How dare Saegar accuse her of being a coward, simply because she cared about her father? How could he understand how she felt? He hadn't seen his own father from the time he was six.

Not that Saegar could be blamed for that, she admitted to herself. He'd had no choice about going into exile. He'd been forced to leave behind the home he clearly loved, and his heritage as well. That had to have been terribly hard. Especially since among his own kind he'd be considered a—

Beth frowned, puzzling over the question. Prince? Heir to the throne? She wasn't really sure what Saegar would have been in Pacifica. But one thing she knew for sure. He'd be a leader. His tendency to give orders was clearly ingrained—as was his unwillingness to compromise.

A few more days, that hadn't been too much to ask for, had it? She knew he was in a hurry to return to

Pacifica, but was he that anxious that he didn't want to spend just a couple more days with her? To talk? To get to know each other better and to—

Oh, God. She shut her eyes as the truth pierced her. He was right. She wasn't keeping him captive simply to restore her father's reputation. She wanted him for herself. Oh, not as a pet, as he claimed, but as a friend. Someone she could talk to, and argue with. She'd been lonely before Saegar came into her life.

But it didn't matter why she'd done it—the point was, she had no right to hold him captive for any reason. No one had. And a bare hour before dawn, she accepted the truth.

She had to let him go.

There was a hushed quality to the atmosphere when Beth slipped into the hold in the dead of the night. Only the moonlight filtering through the porthole lessened the gloom, making the puddles trailing across the floor glisten like mirrors.

But it wasn't until she was halfway down the stairs that she realized something was terribly wrong—that for the first time, the silence was unbroken by the humming of the pump. Her glance flew toward the tank. The water was completely still.

Her heart jumped in alarm, her grip tightened on the railing. "Oh, God," she breathed. "Something's happened. Please don't let him be dead."

She rushed down the rest of the stairs, unheeding of the slippery footing, intent on getting to Saegar as quickly as possible. She'd reached the bottom and started toward the tank when a broad, masculine form loomed out of the shadows in front of her.

Beth instinctively recoiled, a startled shriek rising in

her throat, but lean fingers wrapped around her upper arm, holding her in place.

"Ah," a deep voice said menacingly. "It is you I have caught."

Beth stopped struggling. She stared up into the face above her. "Saegar?" she said uncertainly.

Even the moonlight couldn't soften the hard set of his features as he replied, "Aye, Saegar."

He was tall, so tall that she had to tilt her head back to meet his eyes. Her bewildered gaze quickly flickered away from his forbidding expression to scan his broad shoulders and muscular chest. To drop down past his narrow waist to...

"You have legs!" she blurted. "And—other things."

Her gaze jerked back up, a flush warming her cold cheeks. That brief glance had informed her that along with his new limbs, Saegar had all the usual human, masculine equipment as well. On a very large scale.

"Aye, I have legs," he agreed, and deliberately stepped closer, his sardonic gaze locked with hers. Then, with a quick tug, he whirled her around. Yanking her back against his chest, he locked his arm firmly around her waist. "No longer am I a prisoner in that tank."

Beth's heart pounded harder as he pulled her more tightly against him. He was naked all right.

"But how—what—" She broke off, not sure what she was trying to ask, much less how to say it. She turned her head, her hair brushing against his chest as she looked back up over her shoulder into his face. "Where did your legs come from?"

Cold amusement gleamed in the eyes looking down at her. "I have always had legs. All Pacificans—even meremer—are born with legs. It is not until they are put into the sea that they experience 'the change' and grow their tails. I had legs until the age of six, when I swam off from Pacifica with Bali.''

"You never told me that."

"You never asked."

No, she hadn't, Beth realized. She'd just assumed that meremer babies popped out into the water with tails—like little guppies. But to say so now, seemed horribly rude. Possibly even dangerous.

Still, to find out that she was wrong—that he'd had legs beneath his scales all this time—was disconcerting, to say the least.

"But you told me you could not change."

"Nay, I told you that I am one of the cursed ones. That we are as we are. For the cursed ones, the change is absolute. Once our tails are gone, they will never grow back. Our gills seal up as well, so we cannot breathe beneath the water.''

She felt his chest expand as he drew a deep breath, his voice growing rougher as he added, "If such happens while away from Pacifica, then the cursed ones are doomed never to return home. A fate I now share.''

The final words escaped on a harsh whisper that caused the hairs to rise at her nape. His warm breath brushed against them as he added grimly, "For hours, I sat in the sun, burning away my scales. And then I worked these cursed legs until I could hobble about—hide in the shadows like a crab beneath a rock, while I waited for someone to come down those stairs—to unlock that door—so I could escape. How fortunate," he added silkily, "that the one to do so should be you.''

Fortunate for whom? The words hovered on Beth's tongue, but her throat was so tight she could hardly swallow, much less force out the question. Surely he meant fortunate because she was easier to handle than any of the men.

"I realized you were right and I was wrong. I—I was coming down to help you," she finally managed to croak. "I even told Anne I was going to do something that—that might get Dad upset, but she says he's better—that I should do whatever I needed to. But now—Saegar, you can't leave now. Where will you go? How will you survive? You've already gotten badly hurt once in the ocean, and your wound is barely healed. What if it happens again?"

He gave a humorless laugh. "This time, with you as my hostage, I do not believe Ralph will be so quick to spear me."

"*Ralph* speared you?" Beth repeated, so shocked by the news that she clutched at his arms, still locked around her waist. "I didn't know that."

"Did you not? It appears there is much you were unaware of," he said almost pleasantly—but with a note in his voice that told her he didn't believe her in the least. "But it matters not now."

He slowly began moving toward the staircase.

"Saegar, wait!" Beth said desperately. "If you take me up on deck, naked like you are, it won't be only the Delanos who will come after you, but anyone who catches sight of us."

The conviction in her voice must have gotten through, because he paused to consider what she said.

"You are right, Beth Living Stone," he finally conceded. But instead of releasing her as she'd expected, he began to move deeper into the shadows, dragging her with him.

"Where are you going?" she asked, her voice squeaking a little with alarm. Again she tried to resist, but his arm clamped tighter around her waist, until she felt he was squeezing her in two.

He didn't answer. He just kept walking, forcing her to stay with him, until they reached the door of the storage room.

He opened it and pushed her inside. Beth stumbled forward, then regained her balance and whirled around.

His large frame, silhouetted by the moonlight behind him, filled the doorway. His face was in shadow, but she could still see the faint gleam of his eyes as he stared down at her. Beth swallowed convulsively as he propped a shoulder against one side of the doorjamb, and casually placed his hand against the other, barring her escape.

He spoke suddenly, making her jump. "Open that," he ordered, and gestured at the locker behind her where Ralph kept his extra clothes. "Hand me some breeches."

"Breeches?"

"Pants."

Beth wasn't about to argue with that fantastic idea. Hurriedly, she opened the locker, pulling out a pair of tan pants.

He rejected her choice. "What good are those for concealment in the darkness? Give me black," he growled impatiently.

He had a point, Beth thought silently. Obviously he hoped the dark clothes would prevent him being seen at all. She found a pair of Ralph's black jeans, and held them out.

Saegar took a step toward her—then sucked in a harsh breath as another fiery pain shot up his leg. Sweat beaded his brow. He clenched his jaw, fighting to endure the sporadic cramping of his leg muscles caused by the unaccustomed pressure of his weight. Walking was difficult. Standing still for any length of time was even worse. Balancing on one leg to don the pants would be agony.

He glanced at the little female, who stood waiting with the pants extended. Bathed in the silvery moonlight, she looked like a statue, still and unmoving. Her silence, even more than her eyes—big and black in her white face—told him how fearful she was.

His mouth curved in a ruthless smile. Good. It would make her more acquiescent to his demands. He gestured to his feet. "You claim you want to help me, Beth Living Stone," he said grimly. "So do so now."

He half expected her to argue, but she didn't say a word, simply knelt down to help him. He leaned back against the doorway, bracing his hand against the opposite side of the frame to keep his balance as he laboriously lifted one foot then the other so she could slip the pants over them. Once that was done, he yanked them up to his waist as he ordered, "A shirt."

She obediently turned to paw through the locker again. A black sweatshirt—too tight across his shoulders and chest to zip up—was the best she could do. Saegar gave a dissatisfied grunt at the fit of the garment, but he left it on. Inadequate though it was, it at least covered his back if not his chest, and would make him harder to see when they crossed the deck.

He pointed at a bulky roll of canvas he'd left next to the door. "Give that to me."

Beth wanted to ask what the canvas was for, but a quick glance at his expression dissuaded her. Although the roll was rather heavy, she managed to lift it from the floor and Saegar immediately took it from her, slinging it over his broad shoulder. Holding it in place with one hand, he laid his other arm across her shoulders, tucking her close to his side to prevent her escape. "Now we go."

Beth had no idea how they'd make it up the stairs. When they reached them, Saegar paused and she stumbled to a halt beside him, looking anxiously up into his face. His teeth were clenched, sweat gleamed on his brow. He dropped his arm from around her shoulders but before she could move away, he grabbed her long hair, wrapping it around his fist.

Beth squeaked at the unexpected tug on her scalp. "What are you doing?" she asked, her eyes going even rounder.

"Ensuring you don't escape me."

"I wouldn't—"

"No," he stated flatly, cutting off her protest. "You won't."

He stepped in front of her, the canvas still draped across one shoulder. Placing his hands on the rails he began climbing awkwardly, using the powerful muscles in his arms to spare his legs as much as possible. Beth was forced to stay close to his back, or risk being yanked painfully forward by his grip on her hair. Any second she expected Saegar to tumble backward—taking her with him, no doubt—but he kept going. Awkwardly but steadily he climbed, stopping only once to rebalance the canvas still draped across his shoulder and back.

Beth gave a sigh of relief when they finally reached the narrow landing at the top. Saegar released her hair, but immediately grasped her arm, pulling her in front of him to face the door. "Release the lock."

Beth fumbled through the combination with Saegar literally breathing down her neck. Her hands felt clumsy, almost numb and her first attempt to open the lock failed. Her second failed, too.

Saegar pressed closer, his warmth heating her back as he gave her an admonishing shake. "Don't try my patience," he rasped menacingly.

"I'm n-not—I'm n-nervous—" she stammered.

"Good."

The word was filled with bleak satisfaction. Despite the cold in her hands and feet, sweat trickled down between Beth's breasts. Taking a deep breath, she began again, forcing herself to concentrate. Three spins to the left. One to the right. Two more back again. The lock clicked.

Wrapping his arm around her shoulders, Saegar shoved the door open and stepped out onto the deck with her. The cold, tangy breeze, heavy with mist, rushed to greet them. Beth shivered as it dewed her face and hair, causing small damp tendrils to curl tightly around her temples. Saegar's arm tightened around her, and a shudder ran through his big frame.

She glanced up at him. His head was thrown back, and a look of almost painful relief crossed his face as he inhaled the damp, thick air. Then he started toward the rail.

Once again, he forced Beth to stay with him. His arm felt heavier across her shoulders; he seemed to have more difficulty walking. The ship pitched sharply. They staggered, almost fell, but managed to stay on their feet, clinging to each other for balance. Saegar cursed, a long string of epithets gleaned from scattered coasts around the world and he leaned even more heavily on her.

Then inhaling sharply, he straightened, urging her forward again. "Hurry," he said between gritted teeth. "The dawn is breaking."

He was right. The darkness was fading to a pearly

gray as the sun's rays stretched up beyond the dark horizon. The ship rolled again, propelling them forward.

They landed against the railing with a drunken lurch, Saegar pressed so tightly against Beth's back that the polished brass dug into her stomach. She looked down at the waves breaking against the ship, watching as they rolled playfully this way and that. Her head began to swim. She tried to push away, but Saegar didn't budge. She was caught, Beth realized with a flutter of panic—trapped between Saegar and the deep blue sea.

Her heart beat faster when she felt him shifting behind her. He eased the canvas off his shoulders and into his arms. With a sudden movement that took her by surprise, he threw it over her head into the water.

Automatically, Beth watched the canvas fall. It hit the water with barely a splash, and floated gently. Slowly— so slowly—it began to unwrap, as if an unseen hand were carefully parting its heavy folds. The silvery dawn light was spreading, coloring everything in shades of gray, but Beth glimpsed a golden glitter against the cloth. Then a hungry wave swept forward to swallow it completely, leaving nothing to be seen but the glassy sea.

"What *was* that?" she gasped, turning involuntarily to look up over her shoulder at Saegar's stony face.

His gaze was still fixed on the water. "That was the evidence that kept me captive," he said slowly. "The final proof of who and what I am—was. The cocoon of my tail."

A man shouted in the distance. Another member of the crew answered. Saegar turned his head to look down at her. A chill chased along Beth's spine. In the gray morning light, his eyes were an icy blue.

Beth swallowed. Feeling wretched, she searched for

some sign of relenting in his bleak expression. "Saegar, I'm sorry. I never intended this to happen."

He didn't answer. His mouth compressed in a thin, merciless line, and he took hold of her arms.

Instinctively, Beth clutched at his shoulders, trying to maintain her balance as he lifted her up on her toes. She could hear more shouts and the sound of footsteps rushing toward them, but somehow she knew the men would arrive too late to help her.

"Saegar, please don't." She gasped, as he raised her higher and her feet left the deck. "I'll make it up to you. I promise."

He didn't answer. *This is it,* she thought, looking into his pitiless face. *He's going to throw me overboard.*

She shut her eyes and hung there in his tight grasp, heart hammering, her lips parted in quick panting breaths as she waited to be tossed into the cold sea.

Instead a hard, branding kiss was pressed to her mouth.

Her eyes flew open in shock—and at that moment Big Mike and one of the crewmen grabbed Saegar's arms, while Little Dougie yanked her from his grip.

"Yes, Beth Living Stone," Saegar vowed, still keeping his gaze locked on hers as more men surrounded them. "You will."

Chapter Eleven

Thirty minutes later, Beth was standing next to her father's bed, anxiously scanning the faces of the people gathered in his room. Her gaze traveled from Captain McDugald's stern countenance, to her father's confused yet alert expression, to Anne's curious one, before finally coming to rest on Saegar's impassive features.

He stood apart from everyone else with one shoulder propped against the wall and his arms folded in that subtly arrogant manner she knew so well. His previous anger appeared to have cooled. Now he merely looked bored, as if the dealings of the "dirt dwellers" around him didn't concern him in the least.

Biting her lip, Beth glanced back at her father. He was frowning as he, too, studied Saegar from his ruffled hair, to the ill-fitting sweatshirt and jeans, down to his bare feet. His frown deepened. "Who is this man?"

"I have no idea who he is, sir," Captain McDugald declared, before Beth could answer. "The men saw him holding Miss Elizabeth on deck, and rushed over, thinking she needed help. Frankly, sir, it's my belief that he's a stowaway."

"He's not a stowaway," Beth protested. "He's—"

"Not technically, anyway," Ralph interjected loudly from the doorway, cutting her off as he entered the room.

Carl glanced over at him, raising his brows. "What do you mean, not technically?"

"Actually sir—" Ralph paused, his pale eyes widening as his gaze alighted on Saegar. Even from across the room Beth could see the shock on Ralph's face before he quickly regained his composure. Clearing his throat, he repeated, "Actually, sir, I'm sure this is all a minor misunderstanding. Why don't you let me take him to my cabin? I'll discover what's going on and—"

"No!" Beth put in swiftly. "He's not going with you. You're not going to hurt him again."

"Elizabeth!" Carl exclaimed in surprise, while Saegar glanced at her sharply.

Ralph's gaze jerked around to meet hers. His eyes narrowed. "Listen, Elizabeth—"

"No!" She glared at him, then turned toward the captain. "Saegar isn't a stowaway at all. I invited him onboard *The Searcher*."

It seemed to Beth as if the entire room went still. Her stomach clenched as everyone looked at her.

"For goodness sake, what is this all about?" Carl demanded. "Why on earth did you invite this man aboard ship and why have you kept his presence such a secret?"

"It's a little complicated...." Beth took a deep breath to steady herself, then continued, "You see, Saegar is—was—the one in the tank."

The captain and Anne looked perplexed, but her father's eyes widened, and his cheeks paled. "What?"

Beth stepped closer to the bed to take her father's

hand. Her fingers were still cold from her excursion up on deck, yet his felt even colder. She wrapped her hands comfortingly around them, as she told him gently, "The whole thing was a hoax, Dad. There is no—unusual creature—down in the tank. It was just Saegar."

"That's a lie!" Ralph declared, an angry flush rising under his skin. "That is—he was in the tank, but—"

"That's enough, Lesborn," Carl said sternly.

"But, sir!"

"I said that's enough!"

Ralph stiffened, but remained silent, pressing his full lips into a thin, angry line.

Carl looked back at his daughter, his expression hurt and confused. "But why would you do such a thing?"

Beth stared at him helplessly, not sure what to say. "I just wanted for you to be happy for a while," she finally admitted, knowing that, at least, was the truth.

"I'm happy, daughter," Carl protested. "Why would you believe any differently?"

Anne cleared her throat. Stepping closer to Beth, she put her arm around the younger woman's shoulders. "Maybe because you're always saying how hurt you are that your old colleagues have shunned you, Carl," Anne said, giving him an admonishing look over her glasses. "Maybe because she hasn't been happy, being dragged all over the world gathering legends of mermaids—of all impossible things—just so she can spend time with you."

"Is that true, Elizabeth?" Carl looked back at her, the hurt on his face replaced by concern. "If so, then all you had to do was say so. There was no need for you to perpetuate such an elaborate hoax, and even involve my assistant in the scheme."

Ralph raked a hand through his hair in frustration. "But I wasn't—"

"Don't deny it please, Lesborn," Carl said coldly. "It's obvious you were involved. And although your motives might have been pure, I must say I am deeply disappointed you'd be a party to such a fraud."

Ignoring Ralph's sputtering protest, Carl turned his head to look sternly over at Saegar. "And where do you come into this, young man? Are you some kind of con artist?"

"No! Saegar was against the whole thing from the very beginning," Beth said quickly with perfect truth. "He just did it because—" She hesitated, not sure how to explain Saegar's involvement without causing more trouble. "Because—"

"Because I am her mate," Saegar declared in his deep voice.

Beth nearly choked at this unexpected contribution, while everyone else looked at Saegar in surprise.

Ralph's eyes appeared ready to pop out of his head. "He can t-talk!" he gasped, stuttering in astonishment. "He can speak English!"

Carl stared at him. "Why should that surprise you?"

"Because—"

"Because Saegar isn't from around here," Beth interrupted before Ralph could finish. "Saegar's from—from Finland."

"Ah, now I understand. A foreigner, are you?" Carl gave Saegar's outfit a reappraising glance. "Well, that explains a lot. I thought I caught an accent."

"Yes, and he gets words confused sometimes," Beth said, seizing on the convenient explanation. "What Saegar meant to say is that he's my—er, my boyfriend."

Saegar stiffened and frowned at her.

"I am a man, not a boy," he corrected her flatly, then looked at Carl. "We are betrothed."

Beth's eyes widened. Betrothed! What was he doing? Was he trying to help her? Or make things worse?

She glanced at her father and watched helplessly as the surprise on his face turned into pleased excitement.

Anne looked pleased, too. "So where did you two meet each other?" she asked chattily, clasping her hands together.

"At sea," Saegar told her.

"Yes, we were like those ships that pass in the night," Beth said, trying to prevent Saegar from complicating matters further. "Except—well, it wasn't night and we didn't quite pass. Saegar was on his way home, but I—persuaded him to travel with us for a while and we ended up—" she spread her hands in a helpless gesture "engaged."

"Like hell you did!" Ralph burst out, the ugly flush mottling his pale face turning even darker. He glanced wildly from Carl, to Anne, to the captain and back to his employer.

"Good God, can't you see what's happening here?" Raising a shaking hand, Ralph pointed in Saegar's direction. "Can't you see this—this creature isn't like us? That he's an animal. A freak! A—"

"Lesborn!" Carl said, shock and anger in his voice. "This man is my daughter's fiancé!"

"He's not her fiancé! He's not even a man! He's—" Ralph glanced imploringly at Beth. Seeing her stony expression, his own face twisted in disgust. "Ah, hell, what's the use?" he said angrily, and slammed out the door.

A long silence filled the room.

"Goodness!" Anne finally said, shaking her head as she glanced at Carl.

"I told you that man was unstable," Captain Mc-Dugald stated, his white brows beetling in a stern frown.

"It seems you were right. I never knew Lesborn was so high-strung—and prejudiced against the Finns," Carl replied, his face troubled.

He looked at Saegar, and his expression lightened a little. "Please accept my apologies for my assistant's ill-considered remarks, Mr.—" He paused, his brow wrinkling as he tried to remember. "Pardon me, young man, but is Saegar your first name, or your last?"

For a brief second, Saegar's gaze met Beth's and she saw a sudden gleam light the somber blue depths. Her pulse leaped in alarm as he straightened and threw out his chest.

"Saegar is my given name," he announced. "Yet I am also known as Saegar the Lus—"

"Smith!" she interjected hastily. "He's Saegar Smith!"

Carl winced. "For goodness sake, Elizabeth, there's no need to shout—or keep interrupting. Give the poor man a chance to speak for himself."

"Aye," Saegar agreed, giving her a reproving glance. "Let me speak for myself, Beth Living Stone."

"Fine," Beth said grimly. She was more than willing to do that—but not until she discovered what Saegar planned to say next. Things hadn't been going well to begin with, but now—thanks to Saegar's contribution—they were getting completely out of hand.

"If you'll excuse us," she said to the others, "I need to talk to Saegar a minute. Alone."

Marching over to him, she grabbed his hand and

tugged him toward the bathroom. His gait was slow, but he went with her willingly enough.

"Now," Beth said, once they were inside with the door shut firmly behind them. "What was that all about out there?"

Saegar ignored the question, too busy glancing around the small room with interest to bother to reply. "What place is this, Beth Living Stone?"

"It's a bathroom. The place where we bathe."

His brows lifted as he stared at the porcelain sink. "That is where you bathe?"

"Yes—no, of course not." She gestured impatiently at the glass doors behind him. "In there."

Saegar opened the frosted glass to peer inside and shook his head. Shutting the door again, he caught sight of the little blue dish on the sink.

Beth returned to her original question as he lifted a carved rose and sniffed it. "Now, what was that— Hey!" She yanked his hand down as he held the rose to his parted lips. "That's soap, not food."

"Soap?" Saegar frowned down at the plump, smelly little flower on his palm.

"Yes. Heck, for someone who won't even try tuna…" Just to be on the safe side, she took the soap away from him and put it back in the dish. "Saegar—"

"Ah, you have fleurouva." He stroked a creamy petal of another flower growing on a small shelf. "I have seen these on an island near Japan."

"Yes, well, we call them orchids. Anne's an amateur horticulturist and grows them everywhere she can on the ship. Now, please, Saegar…" Impulsively Beth touched his arm to gain his attention. "Listen to me. Why did you tell my father that ridiculous lie? That we're betrothed?''

He fastened his intent gaze on her and Beth almost backed up a step. She'd wanted his complete attention, but now that she had it she felt strangely uneasy. For just an instant, she thought she glimpsed the anger he'd displayed during his escape deep in his eyes.

Suddenly the room seemed much too small, and Saegar much too large.

Yet, his voice held no hint of anger as he replied, ''Why is your tone so heated, Beth Living Stone? Did not the news of our *ridiculous* betrothal help distract your father from the loss of his creature?''

The touch of acid in his voice made Beth flinch. ''Yes—no, I'm not sure whether it helped or not,'' she admitted. ''He's going to be terribly disappointed when he discovers our engagement is false.''

''Nay, he will not,'' Saegar said casually. ''Because it is the truth. We will marry, and thus set his mind at rest.''

''What!'' Her heart jumped into her throat. ''We can't do that—''

''Aye, we can—and we will. Unless—'' his tone hardened ''—you were telling an untruth once again. You said you would make it up to me—did you not, Beth Living Stone?—for the loss of my tail. This you can do by marrying me.''

''But how will that help?''

''You have told me that marriage will give me legal status if I am forced to enter your country. It will give me standing with your father as well, and divert his mind for a time from his search.''

''But—''

''He has not abandoned his hunt,'' Saegar said

bluntly. "He is too set in his ways to do so. Bali was such a one also—unable to turn aside once his course had been set. The news of our betrothal—and joining—will only divert your father's mind for a time. Nor," he added coldly, "is your Ralph deceived. Despite my legs, he knows what I am, and the riches he can gain if he can yet prove it is so. But if I am your mate he will not dare to gainsay me even if I demand that your ship return from whence it came."

"Is that what you plan to do?" Beth asked. "Head back toward Pacifica?"

"Aye."

"But if you can't enter Pacifica now that you've... changed, what good will going back do?"

He reached up to the medallion around his neck and fingered it thoughtfully. "Because even though I cannot return, Beth Living Stone, I need to find someone I can trust to return this medallion to my people. There is a better chance of finding such a one in the waters near my...home."

The bleakness in his face as he said the word home made Beth feel terrible.

"So what say you? Do you agree to be my mate?"

Beth sighed. Everything he said made sense—and even if it hadn't, she admitted silently to herself, she doubted she could say no after all she'd put him through. Because of her, he'd been forced to give up everything. His home, his family.

Her gaze dropped to the medallion around his neck. "Yes," she agreed in a low voice. "I owe you that much at least."

"Aye, you do."

"But it will be a marriage in name only," she added, looking up into his face again, determined to make things perfectly clear. "And *marriage* is the word to remember here. I don't want to hear any more talk of mating." Just saying the word made her feel kind of—squirmy inside.

Again, Saegar pinned her with his gaze. "Why not?"

"Well—because it's not a word my people use."

"What word do you use?"

"I don't use any word."

He lifted a brow. "So how do you describe it when a man places his—"

"I don't describe it!" Beth interrupted, her cheeks burning. "Just—oh, just never mind!"

"If that is your wish," Saegar murmured. "Now let us return to tell your father that you have agreed to become Beth Living Stone Smith."

"Good lord," Beth muttered.

Carl, who'd been resting back against his pillows, sat up abruptly as they came back into the room. Captain McDugald straightened, and Anne, standing beside the bed with a glass of water in one hand and a pill in the other, smiled expectantly.

"We have something to tell you...." Beth began.

"We wish to be mated," Saegar said. "Immediately."

Chapter Twelve

When Saegar said immediately, Beth discovered, immediately was what he meant. He planned for them to be married that very afternoon.

Anne was obviously thrilled at the news, and hustled Beth to her room. "We need to find you something to wear, dear," she declared, and as soon as they entered, threw open the doors to Beth's closet to survey the colorful array inside.

Beth collapsed on the couch beneath her window, wondering how things had escalated to this point. Was she really getting married? Was it possible? And to Saegar, of all people?

Apparently so.

Saegar had gone off with the captain, who'd offered to help him find some clothes more appropriate for the occasion when Beth had admitted his wardrobe was scanty—to say the least. And Anne had quickly volunteered to help Beth.

Beth watched as the older woman slid the hangers

holding her dresses rapidly along the rod. Yes, that was the problem. Everything was happening too quickly. She needed to slow things down a little.

"Maybe this is all too much for Dad, Anne," she said. "Maybe he's not up to all this and we should wait."

"Nonsense, dear, of course he is. Meeting your Saegar has been a shot in the arm for him." Anne pulled out a pink chiffon formal, frowned at it, and shoved it back on the rod. "He desperately wants to see you settled in case anything happens to him. And of course, he's hoping for grandchildren as well...."

Good lord, Beth thought, involuntarily pressing a hand against the butterflies that suddenly fluttered in her stomach. *Saegar's children.* Her mind filled with the disconcerting images of blue-eyed babies.

"But Dad doesn't even know Saegar," she said weakly. *Didn't know what he is—or rather, was.*

"He trusts your judgment, dear. He and your mother married after they'd only known each other a week, you know." A yellow dress caught Anne's eye—but was banished back to the rod as she added absently, "And anyone can see how much you love Saegar...."

How much she loved Saegar? Beth nearly laughed—hysterically—at the absurdity of the comment. She didn't love Saegar. That was ridiculous!

"All your father wants is your happiness," Anne added, and turned to look at her. "Surely, you know that."

Beth raised her brows. "Then he's not disappointed that I'm not marrying Ralph?"

"Heavens, no," Anne said, turning back to the closet. "Oh, he thought at one time that you and Ralph might make a match of it, but I told him that would never happen."

Beth gave her a sidelong glance. "Why did you think that?"

"You always drew away whenever Ralph tried to get close to you." Pulling out a white sundress, Anne studied it thoughtfully. She laid it on the bed and turned back to the closet. "And, of course, Ralph never looked at you the way your Saegar does."

"What do you mean?"

Anne glanced at her again. Abandoning the dress hunt for the moment, the older woman pretended to fan her face with her hand. "You know what I mean! Talk about your burning glances!"

Beth winced. Little did Anne realize that the "burning glances" Saegar directed her way, weren't caused by passion, but anger. Not only did he blame her for luring him onto the ship in the first place, he was also furious that she'd reneged on her promise to release him when she'd said she would. If she hadn't done that, he wouldn't have lost his tail and thus any hope he had of ever returning to Pacifica.

Nor did he appear to trust her not to break her word again—hence the hasty wedding. Not that she blamed him. She had lied to him, and for that she was truly sorry.

So filled with penitence—and helplessness—she let Anne pick out her dress, and style her hair, following each of her suggestions without argument. And in less time than she would have thought possible, Beth found herself standing on the gently rocking deck, Saegar at her side, as the captain began the familiar ceremony that would bind them together as man and wife.

"We are gathered here today, to unite this man and this woman...."

It's not a real marriage, Beth kept reminding herself

as the captain's voice drifted off on the afternoon breeze. In fact, the ceremony—the whole setting—seemed like something out of a dream, rather than anything based on reality. The brilliant blue sky dotted with a few fluffy white clouds, remnants of the recent storm, looked too perfect. The light wind that flirted with the flared skirt of her sleeveless white dress and playfully freed a strand of her hair from the twist on the top of her head felt too warmly beguiling. Even the orchid trembling in her hands—Anne's donation to the proceedings—was too flawless, with each soft white petal curving gracefully outward from a blushing pink core.

Yes, it all was too perfect—and so strange, Beth thought as she glanced around. Even the people gathered around looked different. Her father, sitting in his wheelchair, had a satisfied smile Beth had seldom seen before, while the rarely emotional Anne stood behind him with sentimental tears in her brown eyes. Ralph was conspicuously absent—although Beth knew he'd apologized to her father for his outburst and immediately been forgiven—but the Delano brothers were there. Little Dougie wore a disapproving expression, and Big Mike as always seemed surprised, his mouth agape as he stared fixedly at Saegar's legs. Every crew member who wasn't on duty was there as well, wearing unusually solemn expressions.

They all looked oddly unfamiliar. But most unfamiliar of all was the man by her side.

Beth slid a sideways glance at Saegar from beneath her lashes, studying the clothes the captain had found for him to wear. A long-sleeved white shirt that fit snugly across his shoulders and deep chest; black jeans that fit equally as snugly across his narrow hips. Beth's gaze moved down to his feet. She was wondering if

wearing black deck shoes felt as weird to him as she
suspected, when Saegar gently removed the orchid from
her grasp.

Startled she glanced up, her empty hands hovering for
a moment in midair before twisting nervously together.
Saegar tucked the flower behind her ear. The tantalizing
sweet smell of it drifted over Beth, mixing with the salty
sea air, as he wrapped his hands around hers.

She stared blindly ahead at his white shirt until his
grasp tightened in a silent demand. Reluctantly, Beth
raised her gaze to meet his. His eyes looked more ach-
ingly blue than the sky behind his head as he gazed
down at her. The wind tousled his dark hair softly
around his hard, tanned face as he repeated after the
Captain, "I, Saegar Smith, take thee, Beth—Elizabeth
Living Stone, as my lawful wife...."

Beth wanted to look away. She couldn't. She stared
helplessly up at Saegar, barely hearing the promise of
the age-old words so entranced was she by the promise
in his intent eyes.

His voice was gruff, yet firm. Hers was slightly shaky
when her turn came to make her vows, but her eyes
remained fixed on his. It wasn't until Saegar looked
down to slide a ring on her finger that Beth was able to
look away as well.

It was her mother's ring, she realized. A sparkling
diamond surrounded by tiny pearls. Not the most expensive ring her mother had owned, but the one she'd trea-
sured the most. The one Beth's father had given to her
on their wedding day.

The enormity of what Saegar and she were doing—
the big lie they were acting—suddenly struck Beth so
forcibly her hand jerked in his grasp.

"I now pronounce you man and wife!" the captain stated. "You may kiss the bride."

No, he couldn't, she thought wildly. This wasn't right, they were making a big mistake. She looked up at Saegar to tell him so, but at that moment he caught her up against him and the words were lost beneath the crush of his mouth.

His arms tightened to lift her off her feet, and Beth's eyes fluttered closed. She clung to the strong column of his neck as he brushed his mouth slowly across hers, again and again, until her lips felt tingly and swollen. She forgot where they were—forgot about the people watching—until suddenly he broke the kiss and lowered her to her feet.

Dazed, Beth clutched at his shirt as her legs threatened to buckle beneath her. She felt dizzy, her head oddly light.

She stumbled a little as Anne rushed up to hug her. "Oh, Elizabeth, I'm so happy for you!"

She was still feeling dazed as she and Saegar were whisked away to the dining room, where Anne had created a beautiful setting for their reception in a very short time.

Candles flickered on white linen on the tables around the room. Tiny twinkling lights draped the food table, where silver trays filled with salmon, mousse pâté, and cheese points served as a testament to Chef Pierre's skill. He'd even whipped up a spinach-and-cheese ravioli, and thin slices of beef tenderloin in a mushroom sauce.

Yes, once again everything was perfect, down to the smallest detail. Anne had even thought to put Beth's father's favorite CD in the music system, so Frank Sinatra was crooning huskily in the background. *This isn't real,* Beth had to remind herself once again. *Saegar and I aren't in love, and our marriage won't be forever.*

She accepted the hugs and good wishes, joined in the laughter and conversations, but her thoughts remained fixed on Saegar. She glanced at him across the room. A group of men surrounded him, listening to one of his outrageous, killer shark tales with appreciative grins on their faces. Beth sighed in relief. She'd worried that he might be standoffish with the men, or that they might not accept her new husband, but those fears were obviously unfounded.

Husband.

Her heart skipped a beat. *Pretend husband,* she reminded herself. She watched as Anne walked up to him, and he bent down to hear what she said. How handsome he was. How strong. How well he was adapting to his new role.

She realized Anne must have told him to join her, because he began walking toward her as the delicate clinking of silverware against crystal quieted the room. Her father was calling for a toast.

She gave a small shiver of awareness as Saegar reached her side, and put his arm around her shoulders. That warm, hard arm seemed to burn through her dress as Saegar hugged her to him and nuzzled her hair, just like a real bridegroom.

Her father beamed at them from his wheelchair. Beth had never seem him look so happy. His eyes sparkled, a smile curved his lips. He looked more robust than he had in months. *I've done the right thing,* she told herself. *Surely I've done the right thing.*

Her father waited until Anne had handed each of them a flute of champagne, then lifted his glass high. "I'd like to make a toast. To my daughter and her mystery man—

now her new husband. May their marriage be long, joyous and fruitful.''

Beth almost choked—and she hadn't even tasted her champagne yet. Saegar clicked her glass with his, as the people around them were doing, then lifted an eyebrow when she linked her arm around his.

"It's traditional among my people," she said. "To drink from each other's glass."

He nodded, and raised his glass to her lips. "Ah, I see. To make sure the bride and groom do not poison one another."

"That's not the reason!" Beth protested, but could say no more as he tipped the dry, bubbling wine into her mouth. She swallowed and placed her glass against his lips to do the same.

He swallowed, then narrowed his eyes. "Much different than beer—or red wine," he said thoughtfully.

Beth's eyes widened. "How would you know?"

"People often cool their bottles in the ocean. At times I have liberated a few."

Beth wanted to ask him more, but at that moment, Chef Pierre made an entrance. He paraded across the room leading two kitchen helpers who carried the cake he'd made in honor of the occasion. A three-tiered cake elaborately decorated with white frosting and pink roses.

"More soap?" Saegar murmured, leaning close to Beth after the men set the cake down before them, and she'd expressed her thanks to the chef.

Beth shivered at the rush of Saegar's warm breath against her ear. "No—sugar. Actually it's chocolate mint. Not a traditional choice, I suppose, but Chef Pierre knows that it's my favorite."

She picked up the silver knife from the salver, and Saegar immediately removed it from her hand.

"Dull," he declared, testing the blade with his finger.

Beth rolled her eyes. "It's for cutting the cake, not vanquishing sharks.

"No, wait!" she said hurriedly as he turned toward the cake with a look of anticipation on his face. Afraid he might start hacking it to pieces, she added, "We're supposed to do this together, too. Here—give it to me and put your hand over mine."

Saegar did as instructed, and fed her the first bite without prompting, slipping the cake carefully between her parted lips. But when Beth performed the same courtesy for him, he nipped her fingers.

It felt as if a current of electricity shimmered up her arm. Beth looked into Saegar's eyes, and realized he, too, remembered the first time he'd done that, down in the hold.

How far they'd come from that moment. How much had changed between them.

For a long moment, they continued to stare at each other, then Saegar slipped his arm around her waist. "It is time for us to go."

Beth's cheeks flamed at the knowing looks some of the men exchanged, but she didn't argue. Because suddenly she'd just had too much—too much laughter, too many goodwill wishes, too many romantic traditions that in their case didn't mean a thing. She just wanted to get away, out of sight of all the people watching before she—or more likely Saegar—did something to reveal what a farce their marriage actually was.

She bid good-night to Anne and her father and headed to the door, with Saegar right beside her. He didn't say anything as they walked to her room, but Beth found herself chattering nervously.

"It was a nice reception, wasn't it?"

"Aye."

"Anne arranged it—she's really a wonder." Since that was all she could think to say about that, Beth reluctantly moved on to a more delicate subject. "I hope you don't mind sharing my room...."

He slanted her a sideways glance.

"It's fairly large," she added uncertainly. "I'm sure we can manage to stay out of each other's way until you reach Pacifica."

Saegar didn't respond to that comment either, and Beth gave a sigh of relief as they finally reached her door.

She opened it...and stifled a silent groan. She'd escaped from one romantic setting only to stumble into another much more dangerous one. Someone—most likely Anne—had gotten there before them and set the scene for intimacy. The drapes were drawn closed, cloaking the room in privacy. The sweet scent of orchids filled the air from the lush pink plant nestled next to the bucket of iced champagne on the coffee table, and the candles in the antique wall sconces on either side of her bed had been lit. Cupid's conspirator had even turned down the bedspread, revealing inviting white silky sheets.

Taking a deep breath, Beth straightened her shoulders and marched in. She headed straight for the lamp by the small couch, and switched it on in an effort to dispel the soft glow cast by the candles.

"Here we go—this is my room." She walked briskly toward the coffee table, and picked up the bucket and the plant, then carried them both into the bathroom.

Saegar remained in the doorway, his gaze roaming the room as she hurried about. The coverlet at the end of the bed and the puffy chairs around the room were covered in a swirl of blues and grays. The thick carpet beneath his feet was midnight blue, as was the matching cloth strung across the window to shut out the night.

Earlier in the day, he had avoided being confined in a room whenever possible. The walls, he'd discovered, had a tendency to close in on him. Only out on the open deck did he feel he could truly breathe free. Yet, he decided, he wouldn't mind spending the night in this sweet-scented room, decorated in the colors of a stormy sea, alone with Beth Living Stone— Nay, Beth Living Stone *Smith*.

His gaze returned to the bed and his eyes narrowed speculatively. More than big enough, he decided, to accommodate the both of them. He walked in, shutting the door deliberately behind him.

He saw his new wife stiffen, then she walked over to a cupboard against the wall.

"It's been a long day, we both should get some sleep," she said, pulling out a blue coverlet.

Without responding, Saegar sat down on the edge of the bed to remove his shoes. He bent and pulled off one then the other and dropped them on the floor. His socks quickly followed.

He glanced up and caught her staring at his bare feet as she clutched the folded coverlet against her breasts.

He lifted his brows. "So, Beth Living Stone Smith, what do you think?"

Her eyes flashed up to his.

"Do my feet look normal to you?"

"Yes—I mean, they're big—" She broke off, color rising in her cheeks, then said, "You know that they look normal."

He stood up, and was amused by the way she hugged the coverlet tighter. Her eyes looked big and anxious, her face pale with the exception of two spots of pink high on her cheekbones, and the rosy red of her mouth. She'd gnawed anxiously on her bottom lip much of the time during their ''reception'' and it now looked pouty and full.

Saegar's lower body tightened as he stared at her swollen mouth. He kept his gaze fixed on her lips as he slowly began undoing the metal clasps binding his shirt at his wrists. Cuff links, the captain had called them. He released the clasps, and dropped them on a small wooden table by a billowy, blue chair.

She gave a start at the small sound. ''Um, that's good, you're getting…comfortable,'' she said, and turned away to spread the blanket over a small couch against the wall. ''I can sleep on this, and you can have the bed—''

''Nay.''

She straightened abruptly, and turned to stare at him. ''But you're too big for the couch.''

''Aye. I am.''

He began unbuttoning his shirt, and Beth was distracted by the sight of his lean fingers moving nimbly from one button to the next. His medallion was underneath it, she saw as the shirt gaped, and she wondered if he ever took it off.

She forgot the question as he undid the last button, and the shirt fell open completely. No doubt about it, he had the best chest she'd ever seen—scars and all. Broad and deep, with flat masculine nipples a couple of shades darker than his smooth brown skin.

She swallowed, trying to relieve the dryness in her mouth. She'd seen his chest before, of course. Every day she'd gone to visit him. But this was different. He was in her room now. They were married.

And he was a *man*.

Suddenly realizing that she was staring admiringly at his bare torso, she quickly averted her eyes, trying to remember what they'd been talking about. Her gaze fell on the couch. That was it. "But—but where are you planning to sleep then?"

"With you."

"Me!" Her gaze whipped up to meet his.

"Aye. On the bed—the floor." He shrugged out of the shirt, and dropped it on the carpet. "It does not matter where we lie."

"It matters to me!" Beth declared.

"Then you choose."

He reached for the fastening on his pants and Beth quickly reached for the lamp. She paused with her hand on the switch, unsure quite what to do. Her impulse was to turn the light off before he stripped completely...but on the other hand, she'd been alone with Saegar—a naked Saegar—in a dimly lit room last night. Repeating the experience didn't seem like the wise thing to do.

"Saegar, wait!" she said desperately, as he pulled down his zipper.

He glanced at her, raising an eyebrow in silent query.

"I thought you understood—that we agreed, that this wouldn't be a real marriage where we—mate."

"I never agreed to such a bargain," he said, and calmly dropped his pants and shorts.

Beth's heart slammed against her ribs. She tried not to look downward, to keep her eyes on his face. Not to notice the strength in his thick shoulders, the way his broad chest tapered to his narrow hips, or the tight muscles of his stomach. She especially fought not to stare at the masculine marking of hair arrowing down from his navel to his—

She flicked off the light switch. It helped—but not much. The candlelight still flickered over his naked form, making his golden skin glow. Her heart skipped a beat as he put his hands on his hips.

"Saegar…" She tried to sound firm, but somehow a slightly desperate note crept in. "I know I talked about this being a marriage in name only."

He nodded. "Aye. But I have learned, Beth Living Stone Smith, that your words are not binding to you." He started toward her.

"They are this time." The slight halt in his stride added a strange menace to his advancing form. Her pulse raced. "Saegar, stop!"

She held out her hands to fend him off.

He kept coming, his narrowed eyes refusing to release hers. "From the moment I first saw you standing on the bow of your ship, you beckoned me nearer—yet you claim you did not. In that cursed tank, you stroked my arms, my shoulders, my hair—yet you claim you sought only to help me. Now you hold out your hands to me—" He caught them in his. "Yet say you want me to come no closer."

Clasping both her hands in one of his, he held them against his chest. His other hand settled at the back of her neck and he gathered her into the curve of his shoulder.

Blue eyes darkening, he lowered his head until his firm lips were but a whisper away from hers. "I say, Beth Living Stone Smith, that your actions do not suit your words, and it is your actions that I believe."

And his mouth covered hers.

Beth tried to step backward, but the hand at her nape tightened, anchoring her in place. His firm lips nudged hers apart with unhesitating possessiveness. His tongue,

hot and demanding, explored her mouth completely until
Beth grew warm, drugged with passion. Engulfed by the
hot tide of desire he aroused with his probing, wicked
tongue.

The room began to spin. To keep herself from falling,
she slipped her arms around his neck and clung to him
for support.

The kiss went on and on, until her lips felt swollen
and tingly. He tasted so good—like chocolate and champagne. His large body radiated heat, and she pressed
closer, her aching nipples budding through her dress and
rubbing against his chest.

His fingers sifted through her hair, dislodging the orchid he'd placed behind her ear. It fell to the floor, but
she ignored it, could only think of the feel of his hard
body against hers. He tugged at her French twist, combing his hands through it, until her hair tumbled down.

Beneath the fall of hair, she felt his fingers moving
slowly along the buttons of her dress, then it loosened,
slipping down her shoulders. Beth shivered at the feel
of the cool air hitting her bare back. Her eyes opened as
Saegar eased her away slightly to allow the dress to drop
to her feet.

Holding her by the shoulders, Saegar stared down at
her as she stood before him. Her eyes were languorous,
her lips slightly parted. His gaze followed the candlelight
dancing across the feminine curves of her body—the
small, high breasts, the sharp indent of her waist, the
sleek curves of her hips covered by a small scrap of
white silk.

He hungered for the sight, the taste, the feel of her.
Reaching out, he touched one of her tight, rosy nipples.
"Ah, little one. You are wondrously made."

Shyly, she lifted her hands to cover herself but he

caught her close and kissed her again. She groaned into his mouth as his hands slid along her silky skin—down her bare back, beneath her panties to cup her rounded buttocks.

He gathered her into his arms and carried her over to the bed, laid her gently down on the cool sheets. She blinked up at him. She looked dazed, yet passion marked her, too. Her hair was a tousled mane around her small face. Her eyes were dark and heavy with desire. Her mouth—ah, that swollen red mouth that tasted so sweet.

He lay beside her and drew her into his arms to taste those soft lips yet again. He kissed her until she was pliant and yielding in his arms, then he tasted the long smooth line of her throat, nibbled on the tender skin of her neck and shoulder. Saegar felt her tremble as he licked her beaded nipples, and when he drew one into his mouth, her warm arms encircled his neck to pull him closer.

He suckled her leisurely, first one breast then the other. His loins grew heavier at the feel of her nipples—like small, hard berries—pressing against his tongue. She held him tightly, stroking his hair, moaning with aroused passion. But when he began to kiss his way down to the soft skin of her belly, she shifted uneasily, and caught his face between her hands.

He looked up. Her eyes, dark and uncertain, met his. "Saegar—no," she whispered, stroking his cheek softly. "I don't think—"

"Nay, do not think. Just feel."

Beth shivered as he lowered his head again, clutching at his hair as his warm lips trailed slowly back and forth across her abdomen then gradually moved lower still. Her breath caught as he slowly pulled off her white silk panties. His mouth brushed a spot right above her thigh, and her womb contracted in a sharp, warm spasm of desire that made her groan.

His hands circled her thighs, gently forcing them to part, and shyness and excitement rushed through her in an urgent mix. Her muscles tightened, and she shifted again, trying to escape. But he wouldn't allow it, holding her firmly in place.

"I would know all your secrets, Beth Living Stone Smith," he said huskily, his warm breath flowing against her.

And then he touched her with his hands and with his mouth and it was too much—too much pleasure—too much intimacy. She writhed and cried out, tugging at his hair until finally—finally!—he came back up to cover her body with his.

Saegar groaned at the feel of her lying beneath him. Never had he been so close to another. No water lay between their straining bodies, to lessen the feel of her silky skin against his. He felt her slender arms circle his waist. Her hands stroked along his sensitive flanks as he fit his body to the wet, welcoming heat of hers.

Gently but relentlessly, he pressed forward until he felt a small barrier. He halted in surprise as the realization struck. She was yet a maid! He was the first—the only man—to have thus claimed her! A wave of possessive triumph swept through him, and he surged forward, breaching the thin restraint to sink fully inside her.

A small, startled cry burst from her at his movement. He could feel her trembling, her muscles tightening around him with instinctive resistance.

"Be still," he rasped, fighting the urge to thrust as she moved beneath him. He slid his fingers into her hair to cradle her head, and wetness brushed against his fingertips. He realized she was crying, tears trailing silently along her temples into her hair.

Something tightened in his chest. He bent his head to kiss her eyelids, the salt of her tears mingling with the sweet taste of her skin. "Do not cry, little one," he said huskily. "I did not mean to hurt you."

He started to withdraw—but Beth's arms tightened around him to halt the movement.

"No, Saegar," she whispered huskily. "Please don't leave."

He *had* hurt her…but Beth already felt the pain lessening, the aching need growing intense again. Pushing her to explore the feeling of having him so deeply inside her.

Cautiously, she moved her hips—and with a groan, Saegar began to thrust, slowly at first, then harder, deeper, carrying her with him. The rhythm of his body was like the sea, Beth thought hazily. Advancing, retreating—building a wave of yearning that kept rising higher and higher inside her—until suddenly it broke and she convulsed, ecstasy washing through her.

Then Saegar stiffened too, and with a stifled groan, held her to him tightly as he found his own release—and claimed her completely as his.

Later—much later—Beth reached out in the warm darkness. She couldn't help it. She kept wanting to touch him, to make sure he was real—that he was truly lying beside her on the rumpled bed.

Her hand brushed his arm. He caught her fingers and raised them to his lips, nibbling gently. A quiver of renewed need tightened her nipples. Heat pooled low in her belly.

"Saegar…"

"Aye, Beth Living Stone Smith?"

In the night, his voice sounded huskier than usual. Deeper. She drew a deep breath to inhale the fresh, masculine scent of his skin—the muskier scent of their lovemaking. She lazily slid closer to his side, drawn by the compelling heat of his big body.

His arm went around her and she rested her head on his shoulder. She wanted to tell him what a fantastic lover he was. To tell him she'd never known such ecstasy existed. She wanted to tell him that she felt closer to him than she'd ever felt to anyone in the world before.

She reached up to stroke his jaw. Her thigh slid over his. She wanted to tell him everything that was in her heart.

But that wouldn't be wise; not with a marriage of pretense. So...

"Saegar," she whispered instead. "Just call me Beth."

Chapter Thirteen

They'd reached a silent truce with their lovemaking, it seemed to Beth. For the next few days as they traveled back toward Pacifica, Saegar didn't mention the past and she carefully avoided bringing up the topic of the future.

During the nights, they made love insatiably, as if they were truly lovers, intent only on pleasing each other. During the day, Saegar spent his time exploring the ship and the new world in which he found himself. Growing accustomed to his new legs; learning how it felt to be fully human.

It constantly amazed Beth how well he was adapting. And it amazed her equally as much how easily everyone on *The Searcher* accepted him as her husband. Her father, Anne, the captain, all gave him their approval. So much so that when Beth asked her father to turn back, telling him Saegar wanted to "honeymoon" with her on an island he'd found, her father did so without any hesitation.

Even the members of the crew seemed to like Saegar.

Only Ralph and the Delanos continued to regard him with hostility. They couldn't seem to forget, Beth thought with a sigh, what he'd once been.

But Saegar wasn't bothered by their hostility. He was too busy to pay them much attention. The same determination that he'd applied to swimming miles in the tank in order to keep fit, he now used to strengthen his legs. He'd walk around the deck endlessly, then force himself to endure a rigorous series of stretching exercises in an effort to make his cramped muscles more flexible.

At first his gait remained halting, his legs obviously still painful. Sooner than Beth would have expected, however, he'd conquered the pain and acquired a broad rolling stride, legs spread to keep his balance on the rocking ship. Only the barest hint of a limp remained in his left leg as evidence of the transformation he'd undergone at such a cost.

Yet despite his "normal" new appearance, Beth quickly discovered that Saegar was still different from anyone else she knew. A strange combination of vast knowledge and abysmal ignorance.

For instance, he could barely read. It wasn't that he didn't like books; he did, and pored over the ones on her bookshelf by the hour, laboriously making out the words. But since Bali hadn't considered reading an important survival skill—and there certainly hadn't been any books out in the ocean anyway—Saegar's formal education in the subject had ended at the age of six when he left Pacifica.

To Beth, who loved books, this seemed appalling.

On the other hand, Saegar spoke several languages. Her jaw literally dropped the first time she heard him speaking fluent French with a member of the crew.

Saegar turned as the man left, and caught sight of her

dumbfounded expression. His deep chuckle escaped him, and he dropped a kiss on the surprised O of her mouth.

"What? Did you plan to give me lessons in French also, *mon petit poisson,* as you tried to do in English?" he asked, pinching her chin teasingly.

Beth swatted his hand away. Her French might not be fantastic, but it was certainly good enough to recognize "my little fish" when she heard it. Although she had to admit she was completely at sea—so to speak—when it came to the other languages he knew. Greek, Norwegian, Italian, Russian, Chinese, Spanish—he could speak them all, as well as a few lesser known dialects from islands scattered around the globe. Lurking around docks and ships for twenty-five years, she thought wryly, was obviously a great way to become a linguist.

But he certainly wasn't knowledgeable about food. He refused to touch meat at all. Fresh fish and vegetables remained his preferred diet, and he salted everything excessively, which Beth knew enraged her father's chef.

For some odd reason, it seemed to enrage Ralph as well. They all dined together—Carl insisted on it in hopes of easing what he referred to as the "recent unpleasantness" between Saegar and his assistant—but there was no denying the meals were tense.

Yes, Ralph was still a sore spot, Beth thought silently, as they sat down to dine one night. She happened to glance his way and caught a look of contempt on his face as he stared at Saegar across the table.

An uneasy feeling stirred in her stomach. She'd seen the look before, when Ralph had caught her alone one day to try to persuade her to tell her father what Saegar "actually was."

"Carl will believe *you,* Elizabeth," Ralph had assured

her. "Especially if we can get a sample of the merman's blood and have it tested. There's bound to be a difference in his DNA from normal people."

"Forget it, Ralph," Beth had responded through clenched teeth. "Just leave Saegar—and me—alone."

That's when Ralph had turned that hateful look on her. "So he's somehow enthralled you, has he? Fine. I won't bother you again."

And he hadn't…but he or the Delanos were always nearby whenever Saegar went up on deck. And Ralph never missed an opportunity to goad Saegar whenever possible.

So Beth wasn't surprised when Ralph's eyes narrowed as he watched Saegar pour salt over his delicately seasoned filet de sole.

Beneath his moustache, Ralph's full lips puckered as if he'd tasted something sour. Suddenly, he flung down his napkin.

"Savage!" he muttered loudly, and scraped back his chair to storm out of the room.

Anne looked at Beth's father and shook her head. "You're going to have to dismiss that man, Carl. And in my opinion, the sooner the better."

Distressed by Ralph's behavior, Beth glanced at Saegar to see his reaction to the insult, and found his eyes gleaming with deadly anticipation as his gaze tracked Ralph's progress to the door.

He did look savage, she thought silently. And the thought recurred again and again over the next few days. Every so often she'd glimpse something untamed in his eyes, a stalking menace in the lithe way he moved. He was used to living by his own rules. Doing what he chose.

Like a savage, he even hated wearing clothes.

"It will bind my arms, restrict my movements," he'd growl when she'd hand him a shirt to put on. "Why must I don this?"

"Because wearing clothes is part of our culture—almost all cultures," Beth reminded him firmly. "You told me that even on Pacifica people wore clothes, so you really have nothing to complain about. Besides, it will make you less conspicuous."

Her tone wasn't quite as convincing as she added that last bit. The truth was, Saegar couldn't help but be conspicuous—his height, his muscular build, his golden skin and striking features—all ensured he drew attention no matter what he was wearing. And since he wore shorts whenever possible, it wasn't long until his legs were as strong and bronzed as the rest of him.

Yes, he was changing, she thought, looking up from her book to watch him prowling around the deck late one afternoon. She'd settled in a deck chair, but Saegar never sat still for long. He strolled about with his new broad rolling gait looking like a cowboy who'd just gotten off his horse. Ignoring the Delano brothers who were loitering nearby, he stopped to chat with a deckhand who was polishing the brass railing. They spoke in Spanish, so Beth couldn't be sure what they were saying, but she saw Saegar's white teeth flash as he laughed at some comment the other man made.

He looked happy—as happy as she felt—yet she couldn't quite make herself believe it. Oh, he laughed and teased, but every now and then she'd catch him looking at her with that same watchful expression she'd seen down in the tank before he'd ever spoken. As if a chasm lay between them that could never be bridged.

The thought made her throat tighten. How could that be when she felt so close to him? Closer than she'd ever felt to anyone before. A light breeze was blowing, tousling his dark hair and she resisted the urge to go to him and smooth it back, to put her arms around him and hug him as hard as she could.

As if he sensed her regard, Saegar turned to look at her. His eyes widened a little, then narrowed to gleaming slits. Striding over to her, he held out his hand to pull her up from her seat.

"Let's go," he said huskily. "I need a shower."

It was an excuse, Beth knew, to return to their cabin, but she went along willingly. He reveled in showers, taking several a day, and this time he dragged her in with him, clothes and all, before she could escape. She wouldn't have minded, except he liked the water cold—icy, freezing, bone-chilling cold.

She shrieked when he held her beneath the spray, which made Saegar roar with laughter. Then he growled with satisfaction as she tried to burrow against him, seeking the heat his big body radiated constantly.

They ended up making love—as so often happened. He truly was Saegar the Lusty, Beth thought drowsily, as they lingered in bed. The cold showers certainly didn't have any affect on his libido.

Saegar, still naked, had turned on the television, and propped his shoulders back against the headboard to watch whatever programs the satellite afforded. Smiling, Beth stretched luxuriously, then ran her palm up along his muscular thigh.

"You make love like a prisoner on parole," she murmured—and immediately wished she could take the remark back as his muscles stiffened beneath her hand.

Then he shrugged, relaxing again. "You make love like a woman who has been a virgin for too long."

It was Beth's turn to tense. "How is that?" she demanded suspiciously.

"Constantly surprised by the pleasure. A little shy. Rather clumsy—" he grinned and caught her hand before she could hit him "—but very, very eager."

"Oh! You—" Beth tried to pull her hand away, but he wouldn't release her. Instead he kissed her fisted fingers one by one until they relaxed in his grip, and she nestled by his side again.

Saegar's attention returned to the television, but Beth wanted to talk. Not about Pacifica, exactly, but about what he'd be doing now that he could no longer return there. How he now felt—in general terms, of course—about her.

But Saegar had gotten hold of the remote and was flipping rapidly through the channels. He certainly was like a normal human male in that regard, she thought wryly. He didn't stay with any program for more than a few seconds before he was on to the next. Maybe she should call him Flipper, after all.

She sighed, and ran her finger across his hard chest. "Saegar…"

He didn't answer. She looked up at his face. He was staring at the television intently. She followed his gaze and saw his attention had been caught by a swimming meet.

The men were racing freestyle, and Saegar gave a scornful snort as he watched their efforts. "A shark would catch them in less than a quarter league," he told her, and pressed the remote.

Click. Click. Click. He stopped again, this time on the Discovery channel. Divers were retrieving lost treasures from an ancient Spanish galleon that had sunk hundreds of years ago off the coast of Florida.

Saegar raised his eyebrows as he saw the dented silver goblets the people on the program were exclaiming over.

"Why are they so pleased?" he asked, glancing down at Beth. "I know where many ships lie beneath the ocean, with much richer booty than this."

"You do?" Excitement shot through her, and she raised up a little to lean on her elbow. "But why haven't you recovered any?"

"I did not need it," he answered simply.

"So where are they?"

He shrugged. "All over. Many near the lands you call Florida, Spain and China."

Beth frowned. The places he was mentioning were very populated. "Weren't you afraid someone might see you?"

"They saw me at times—they just did not realize I was mer. I never let them see my tail." He paused to watch a diver delicately brush sand away from an ancient gun, then added almost absently, "Except children, of course."

Beth sat upright. Holding the sheet over her breasts, she demanded, "You let children see you were a merman?"

"Sometimes. Not too often," Saegar said. His hard face softened. "One little girl even waved to me, not frightened at all that I was half fish, half man."

"What did you do?"

He raised his eyebrows. "I waved back."

"But weren't you worried she might give you away?"

He shook his head. "Even if she did, who would believe her?" He glanced over at her, a sardonic expression on his face. "Have you never noticed how often children tell the truth, yet are not believed?"

He might be right, Beth conceded silently. She really

didn't know much about kids. But Saegar obviously liked children a lot. He'd made contact, even waved at them. Something he would never do with human adults...would he?

A small prick of jealousy caused her to ask, "Did you wave at women, too, Saegar?"

He slanted her a knowing glance. "You do not need to know all my secrets."

But she did, Beth realized. She wanted to know all about him. But mostly, she admitted silently to herself, she wanted to know what he felt about her.

She studied his rugged profile as he watched the divers on the program hoist up an ancient cannon they'd found. He obviously still didn't trust her; his remark about her knowing his secrets indicated that. But he'd trusted her once. Enough to let her know he could speak. What had made him trust her then?

"Saegar, why did you finally speak to me—that first time down in the hold?"

Something in Beth's voice made Saegar glance at her sharply. Until then, he hadn't been paying much attention to the conversation, but when he met her eyes, he saw that her expression was serious, and maybe a little troubled.

"Why did you start talking to me then?" she asked again. "When you wouldn't before?"

He thought back to that day. He remembered how furious she'd been when he had eaten the piranha, and his mouth curled in a small smile. "I spoke because you said you were giving up. I thought you might not return, and I needed your help."

"I only said that because I was angry. Because you splashed me—for at least the hundredth time." Her slim brows drew down in frown. "And why did you keep doing that?"

"Because it displeased you," he said blandly. "And you displeased me with that constant litany of words. *Wa-ter. Tank. Food. Good boy.*"

"I didn't know you could understand me!"

Amused by the growing indignation on her face, he casually rolled over, pinning her to the mattress with the weight of his body, his legs lying between hers. When she tried to push him off, he caught her wrists in his hands.

Holding them trapped on either side of her head against the pillow, he stared down into her mutinous face. "Some of your speech I enjoyed," he said, then quoted, "What a *handsome* merman you are! So big! So *manly!*"

The absurd way he batted his dark eyelashes, the inflection in his teasing voice, gave the words a sly sexual reference that made Beth flush hotly. "I never said it like that! Like some—some inept flirt trying to pick you up! I never thought of you like that at all."

"Did you not?" he murmured. Looking down into her stormy sea eyes Saegar knew that he could not say the same. Even then—trapped in the tank—he'd wanted her, been resentful of the sexual pull she exerted on him without effort.

In truth, he'd splashed her for the reason he'd given her, but he knew now there had been another reason as well. Because when she was wet, she'd appeared more like his kind—a mermaid. A female he could mate with. Possess and keep with him forever.

He dropped a kiss on her rebellious mouth, then another, ignoring the warning in her flashing eyes. Aye, he'd enjoyed seeing her with her curls dampened, her skin glistening—but he enjoyed getting her wet even more now, in that mysterious female core of her that fit him so tightly; it was as if they became one.

He was already hard from lying atop her, feeling her soft breasts against his chest, his pelvis nestled against hers. The small warm puff of her breath against his throat as she huffed in exasperation, the way she tried to buck him off when she felt him pressing against her, only increased his ardor.

Beth narrowed her eyes. "Oh, no, you don't!" She squirmed around beneath him, twisted her head to the side when he went to kiss her mouth again. "You're not going to insult me—and then expect to turn around and make love!"

He released one of her hands to catch her chin, gently forcing her to meet his gaze. He smiled, his eyelids drooping lazily. "Aye. I am."

And he kissed her panting, outraged mouth until her lips softened and clung to his. Until her hands—freed from his grip—stroked urgently along his back, his flanks, as she fought to bring him closer.

"Saegar," she whispered against his throat, her breathing ragged. Her hands slid up to caress his hair, then down to clutch at his arms. "Saegar—Saegar, please— Now— Oh!"

She arched and threw back her head as she climaxed, her hips rising to press tightly against his. Saegar stared down at her through a haze of passion, then the pleasure flooded him, too, and he groaned, thrusting harder before collapsing beside her.

Beth quickly fell asleep. The television was still on, but Saegar paid no attention to the mute, flickering screen. Instead he leaned on his elbow beside her, studying her still form as dusk shadowed the room.

She lay on her back, her face turned slightly away. His gaze traced the delicate shell of her ear, the feathery fan of dark lashes lying against the innocent curve of her cheek. Her rich brown hair flowed across the pillow, and one of her small hands lay palm upward among her soft curls.

Her other hand clutched the sheet. Even in sleep she'd covered her breasts with virginal modesty. The fluid white silk flowed over her slim figure like liquid ice, revealing the small peaks of her nipples, the tiny hollow in the middle of her concave belly, the feminine mound at the apex of her thighs.

She stirred, turning her head, and his gaze returned to her face. She looked peaceful, content…and a spark of anger flared inside him that it should be so. That she didn't feel the aching need, the constant yearning for him that he felt for her.

His jaw tightened. He'd thought, without ever quite putting it into words, that once he'd possessed her the need would lessen. Instead, it grew stronger every day, every minute he was with her. Even now, he had to fight the urge to awaken her again. To run his finger down the smooth line of her lovely neck and along her fragile collarbone to her shoulder. To stroke and caress her silky flesh until she clung to him, called out his name once more—because only when she was in his arms, clinging to him, did his hungry desire ease.

She stirred again, reaching toward him as she sighed in her sleep. He stared down at her small hand. Gently, he pressed the vulnerable center of her pink palm until her slim fingers curled reflexively around his. Even that slight touch burned through him. He jerked his hand away, cursing beneath his breath as he swung his legs out of the bed and stood up.

He paced to the window and threw it open. Pushing aside the curtain he stared out at the cloudy sky. Another storm was moving in. The sea was restless and he could taste the rain borne on the wind.

When the storm struck would be a good time to leave. Restlessly, he turned away from the window. He should have dived overboard two or more days ago, gone off on his own to return to the cove, to wait there for an opportunity to return the medallion to his people. Ralph and his men watched him still, but that was not what had held him back. Nay, it was the little female who had kept him from his duty.

He stared at her in the dusky light as she lay on the bed. She belonged to him. Again and again, he'd taken her, to prove to her that it was so. He'd thought to punish her with the marriage—to make her care for him, so she'd feel the pain of losing him when he left. As harsh a pain as he'd felt at the loss of his home, his family.

He watched constantly for a sign that he'd succeeded. That she'd accepted him, wanted him as her true mate. Yet she never spoke of the future, nor begged him to stay with her forever. Nay, he'd been a fool to think that she ever would. That she'd learn to want him—not only to satisfy the needs of her flesh, but to satisfy the needs of her heart and her soul as well.

The way he wanted her.

His mouth twisted wryly. Aye, he was the one being punished, remaining by her side. She held him prisoner still, almost as securely as when she'd kept him in that tank. But tonight he would break away, end this subtle yet piercing torment, and return to the lonely sea where he belonged.

And put Beth Living Stone Smith out of his life forever.

Chapter Fourteen

A sudden, sharp pitch of the ship jolted Beth awake a few hours later. For a moment, she was disoriented in the darkened room, but then she felt a cool breeze against her bare shoulders. She looked toward the window and realized it was open. Saegar was standing in front of it, his dark head and broad shoulders framed by the ship's running lights shining through the glass.

He'd gotten dressed, she noticed, in jeans and a black hooded sweatshirt. How odd.

"Saegar?" she said softly.

He glanced over his shoulder at her as the ship rolled again.

Beth groaned. "Heavens, it's starting to blow out there, isn't it?" Another roll of the boat brought another wave of nausea. Making a face, she pressed a hand to her stomach. "My stomach gets so upset when the waves get rough. I'll have a heck of a time keeping anything down when I get pregnant."

He tensed, and swung around to face her. "Are you with child?"

"Goodness, no," Beth said, her eyes widening as the ship heaved again. The nausea was bad enough already without that.

He stared at her for a moment, then his mouth tightened. "Good," he declared flatly.

Beth stared at his shadowed face in hurt surprise. Saegar sounded as if he were rejecting the idea of children—their children—completely.

But even that hurt was nothing compared to the pain that ripped through her as he added almost harshly, "I would not want to leave a child behind, when I leave tonight."

Tonight?

Beth swallowed, trying to loosen the sudden constriction in her throat. "You're leaving? For good?"

"Aye."

Part of her couldn't believe it. Another, greater part, knew she'd been expecting it all along.

Somehow she'd known her happiness couldn't last. Not when the vows they'd taken had no love behind them. They might as well have been written on water, so unsubstantial were they.

Still, she couldn't help asking, "Why tonight?"

"The cove is not far from here. I can swim there in one, mayhap two days' time."

"But I thought you said we'd cruise in the waters around Pacifica until you found someone to pass the medallion on to."

"Aye, but I have reconsidered such a scheme. To bring so many humans close might endanger my people."

Hurt tightened Beth's throat even more. So, despite

his seeming ease with the crew, with her father—with *her*—he still didn't trust humans. Before she could protest, he spoke again. "Besides," he said, "there is no one I trust to return the medallion except the members of my family. They know where the cove is located and perhaps they will seek me there." His eyes held a distant expression as he added, "They cannot all have forgotten me."

Then why haven't they come before? Beth wanted to demand. Why didn't they come to find you during the past twenty-five years?

But she didn't. What good would it do?

Instead, she asked again, "But do you need to leave tonight?"

Her distress must have been apparent in her voice, because he hesitated, his keen eyes searching her face before he slowly nodded. "Aye. The storm has hit. The crew will be busy and if Ralph—" his expression hardened at the name "—seeks to stop me, it will be more difficult for him to do so in the wind and rain."

"But we can take you to the cove on *The Searcher*. There's no need for you to go by yourself...."

Her voice trailed off. Saegar was shaking his head. "Nay, the location of the cove is a secret, known only to my family. I would keep it so."

Again Beth wanted to protest. To say that if Saegar confided in her father, she was sure that he would remove anyone from the ship that Saegar didn't trust. But she didn't say that, either.

She simply couldn't stand to hear that Saegar didn't trust her father. And possibly her, as well.

Besides, his mind was made up. She could tell that by the set of his jaw, the way his eyes had once again turned watchful and wary. No, she had no right to tell him anything, to ask him to take her with him, or to beg him to stay.

She'd stopped him from leaving before, forced him to make a life-altering decision against his will. She wouldn't make that mistake again.

She pushed aside the covers. Grabbing the sheet, she held it against her, dragging it with her as she headed toward the closet. She staggered as the ship rolled again, but made it without falling.

"All right," she told him, feeling his gaze on her back. "I'll help you leave tonight. Right now."

"I do not need your help. Stay here," Saegar told her coldly.

"I'm coming with you," Beth repeated stubbornly as she stepped into the closet. Dropping the sheet, she began to pull on her clothes. Black pants, a soft blue sweatshirt, another sweatshirt over that—this one black like Saegar's.

As she slipped her feet into her sandals, he said again, "Nay. There is no need."

Beth emerged from the closet, her chin lifted high, careful not to look his way in case he realized how upset she was. *She'd never see him again after tonight.* The thought made her want to burst into tears. To wrap her arms tightly around him and never let go.

But she couldn't. From the first moment she'd seen him out in the water, she'd brought nothing but trouble into his life—a life that already had plenty of sorrow to begin with. Now there was only one way to make it up to him. And that was to let him go without recriminations.

But she was determined to be there when he dived overboard. To make sure he got away safely.

"The storm is drawing near," he reminded her as she headed toward the door.

"I won't melt."

"The ship keeps pitching."

"I know that, too." How could she miss it? The way the room was tilting back and forth, she had to hold on to the door frame just to keep her balance.

The silly argument was making her mad. Funny, she'd never known the anger was there deep inside her, but it must have been all along. Because suddenly, it welled up in a hot, seething rush.

She welcomed the emotion. It gave her the strength to follow him out the door, kept at bay the painful grief still trapped inside her.

For some reason, she'd expected him to head toward the bow, but he turned in the opposite direction down the corridor.

"You will get sick from the cold," Saegar said, his voice oddly rough, as he paced by her side.

"It doesn't matter." No, it didn't. Nothing mattered but holding tightly to her anger and staying with him as long as possible—because when he disappeared from sight, the real pain would begin.

"Go back," he growled.

"No! I need to see you leave."

Her voice, louder than she'd intended, had a shrill note that made him glance at her sharply. But Beth averted her face to avoid that searching glance and quickened her pace.

She wouldn't let him know she was hurting, she thought fiercely. That her heart was breaking apart, bit by bit, with each lurching step that they took.

Fifty more steps and he'll be gone and you'll never see him again...forty more steps...thirty more steps...

Her anger was evaporating rapidly. She marched toward the door leading outside, stubbornness more than anything else sustaining her now.

When they stepped outside, Saegar's hard arm came around her to keep her upright. The storm hadn't hit yet, but the cold wind slapped her face. Numbed her cheeks, her nose, her mouth.

That was why her voice sounded thick as she said, "You'd better go quickly."

But Saegar was steering her toward a metal mast near the lifeboats. "Here. Hold on to this."

She did as he ordered, wrapping her arms around it. She didn't know what the pole was for. She didn't care. She didn't even care that the metal was icy cold. She hugged it tightly. It was hard and firm and something to hold on to when he left.

But for now, he still stood at her side, one hand wrapped around the pole over her head, his body bumping hers slightly with the erratic rolling of the ship.

Why didn't he go? she wondered. Why was he hesitating? She laid her cheek against the freezing metal seeking the sharp sting of icy pain. For a few seconds, it made her forget the huge pain in her heart.

Because the numbness, like her anger, was fading, too. Melting under a flood of aching need. She swallowed past the lump in her throat, her eyes burning.

If he didn't leave soon...

"Beth?" His voice was low but reached her despite the rushing wind and the rain. It must be raining now, she thought, because she felt hot drops coursing down her cheeks.

"Little one, are you crying?" He touched her shoulder.

She jerked away from his hand. "No!" Her voice was

muffled by her hand as she wiped the drops away. ''Just go, Saegar.''

''But—''

''Just go!''

Good! He was moving away. She stared at his broad back, his tousled hair, hungry for each last glimpse of him.

But then he paused and turned back to face her. He was frowning as his eyes met hers, his brows drawn down. Then his eyes widened. He moved—whether toward or away from her, Beth couldn't tell—and at that moment a voice rang out.

''Stop right where you are!''

Saegar froze, then his gaze—like Beth's—fastened on Ralph, who stood ten feet away with the Delano brothers behind him.

''Get him,'' Ralph said to Big Mike, and told Dougie, ''You go watch Beth.''

Dougie walked over and grasped her arm, while Big Mike lumbered toward Saegar. But just before the other man reached him, Saegar broke toward the rail.

Big Mike followed doggedly, but Saegar would have escaped if the ship hadn't pitched unexpectedly, throwing him back a step. Big Mike wrapped his arms around him from behind. They swayed together, but Beth could tell immediately that Big Mike wouldn't hold Saegar long.

Ralph must have realized it, too, because he lifted the gun as Saegar sent the other man staggering backward.

''Go, Saegar! Jump overboard! He's going to shoot!'' Beth screamed.

Saegar's gaze flashed to her, then to Ralph. One second Saegar was there; the next, he'd leaped over the rail and was gone.

He's done it! He's safe! Beth thought exultantly.

Then she saw Ralph, rage contorting his face, stride to the rail.

He lifted his gun again. He was scanning the water—pointing his pistol at the waves, at Saegar.

Beth wasn't even aware she'd moved. All she knew was that suddenly she had hold of Ralph's wrist and was yanking frantically on it, trying to get the gun away.

"You bitch!" Ralph snarled, and hit at her with his other hand. The blow landed against her shoulder, making her stagger, but it didn't make her loosen her grip.

Dougie joined the fray. Then Big Mike lunged against them and they hit the rail, still grappling. Ralph lost his balance and toppled overboard, carrying Beth with him.

She was falling—falling—

Beth hit the water with a *whack!* that knocked the air from her lungs. The cold was immediate and immense, the roar of water in her ears frightening. She flailed her arms, but kept sinking down into the dark, swirling depths.

Burning, icy water filled her mouth, her nose. Her lungs.

Her arms twitched feebly then grew still as her muscles weakened. She was going to die, Beth realized. Yet, it wasn't her life that flashed before her blurry eyes, but Saegar's face.

His blue eyes were there—staring directly into hers through the surging water. Just like the first time she'd seen him.

I love you, Saegar, she thought.

And a sudden peace washed over her, carrying her into darkness.

It hurt, coming back to life again. And it was very unpleasant to have Saegar pushing on her chest as he ordered harshly, "Breathe, Beth Living Stone Smith! *Breathe!*"

But his voice was so commanding that she obeyed, and—oh, God—that hurt worse than ever. Air rushed into her lungs while water rushed out of her mouth and nose—burning, painful, utterly gross. She coughed and retched until her throat was raw, turning her head to the side to be sick.

"There, there. You're all better now," Anne's gentle voice said above her, and Beth felt a soft cloth wipe across her mouth.

"Ralph! The Delanos!" she gasped, on a sudden surge of panic.

"Hush, little one," Saegar said. His warm hand brushed her hair soothingly back from her brow. "The captain has them under guard."

He stroked her hair again. It felt so good—so comforting—that Beth lay there limply, just concentrating on breathing, letting the blessed, blessed air flow in and out of her abused lungs.

She would have lain there even longer, but strong arms slid under her head and knees to lift her effortlessly against a hard, smooth chest.

"I will take her to our room," Saegar said above her head. Beth didn't open her eyes—but she didn't need to. She would have known it was him holding her even if he hadn't spoken because of the compelling heat of his body, the fresh enticing scent of his skin.

She buried her face against him as he carried her. She still felt too weak to even put her arms around his neck, but it didn't matter. He was holding her so tightly she couldn't have gotten any closer if she'd tried.

Her eyes fluttered open as he shifted her in his arms

to open the door, but even then he didn't put her down. Under lowered lashes, she stared up at his starkly handsome face, admiring the grim jut of his chin as he carried her across the room.

"Where are you taking me?" she summoned up the energy to ask drowsily.

"To the bath. You are cold. It will warm you."

Only a merman would stick a person who had nearly drowned beneath even more water, Beth thought wryly.

But when he stepped under the warm spray with her—clothes and all—she had to admit it felt heavenly. It relaxed yet revived her. She was even able to stand unsteadily as Saegar stripped her and himself completely, keeping one arm locked around her waist to prevent her from tumbling into a heap.

Then he straightened. Beth shut her eyes, wrapping her arms around his waist and leaning her forehead against his chest as his hands moved gently over her. He washed her completely, his fingers sifting through her hair until her scalp tingled at his warm touch. Her skin glowed with heat as he stroked along her back, her buttocks, her breasts and belly.

Then his big hands slid along her cheeks to cradle her face. He tilted her head back, and stared down into her eyes—his darker and deeper than she'd ever seen them.

Suddenly, he released her to gather her tightly against him. "My love, my own—I almost lost you."

The words were muffled, his lips buried against her hair, but they went straight to Beth's heart. Warmth unfurled inside her, flaring from her chest outward to her fingers and even her toes.

Her toes curled with delight against the tile beneath her feet. She lifted her foot to slide it slowly up his muscular calf. Snuggling closer, she nestled his hard shaft more firmly against her belly and linked her arms around his strong neck.

She pressed her lips against his throat. Her voice was muffled, too, as she said, "Oh, Saegar, I love you so much."

But he must have understood her, because he swung her up in his arms again. He carried her to their bed, and without even bothering to dry their wet bodies, laid her down.

And in an act as old as life itself, he mated with her, claiming her as his once more. Binding her to him—this time, forever.

Epilogue

For twenty-five years Saegar had waited in the lonely sea to be reunited with his family. Yet, he and Beth were at the cove less than twenty-five days when they saw a sail on the horizon.

They weren't standing on *The Searcher,* but on the deck of a new, sleek yacht they'd purchased. A craft big enough to live on; small enough that they could sail it alone.

After Beth's near drowning, Saegar insisted Beth learn to swim. To her delight, the more proficient she became, the more she enjoyed the sea. She began to love to explore the ageless yet ever-changing depths. Especially with her husband by her side to explain its myriad wonders.

They were alone in the cove. *The Searcher* had traveled on—not toward Pacifica but toward the Baja Lagoon where the mighty gray whales gave birth.

"I've always wanted to see the creatures," Anne had

told Beth's father: "And we aren't getting any younger, Carl. We have no time to waste."

To Beth's pleased surprise, her father had agreed. The changes Beth had noticed at the wedding were becoming more apparent every day. He was looking forward to the future instead of dwelling in the past, and the change in attitude seemed to have improved his health. He admitted he felt better than he had in years. So after turning Ralph and the Delanos over to the authorities at the nearest port, *The Searcher* had departed.

But she and Saegar had immediately returned to the cove after buying their new boat. Beth smiled as she remembered how angry Saegar had been when he'd seen the painter had misspelled the name he'd selected for the vessel.

"I would the craft be named after you, but those are not the initials of your name, Beth Living Stone Smith," he'd said, scowling at the curling white letters, *BLISS*, scrolled on the boat's blue hull. "The sign smith made an error."

"Yes," Beth agreed, with a small smile. "But a fortunate one, I think. Those might not be my initials, Saegar, but bliss is what I feel whenever I'm in your arms."

He'd been appeased by that and had taken her in his arms for a kiss. His arms were around her now as they watched the other boat approach. Then, as it came near enough to see the people standing on the other craft's bow, Beth felt him stiffen against her side. She couldn't make out the people's features, but her husband's eyes were keen.

His arm tightened around her shoulders. "It is Kai. And Phoebe."

Beth's eyes widened. She twisted in his hold to look up into his face. "Oh, Saegar, are you sure?"

Saegar nodded. "Aye. They bear the seal." But that only confirmed what his heart had immediately recognized. That the women had his mother's slender form; his father's hair and eyes.

He released her and without hesitation, dived into the water. Beth looked across at the other boat to see the women follow suit. Her eyes burned as she watched the joyful reunion that followed. The three laughed and cried and embraced in the water with the same unquestioning love that as children they must have once shared.

Then everyone came aboard the *BLISS* and Beth met Saegar's sisters and their husbands as well. Beth liked the men immediately—both human as far as she could tell, and she could see by his relaxed expression that Saegar liked them, too.

It was only when he greeted Locan, the son of his father's enemy who accompanied the group, that his watchful expression returned.

The two men stood facing each other with their gazes locked. Both tall, both blue-eyed. One the new leader of Pacifica; the other an exile from his home all his life.

They eyed each other unflinchingly, then Locan's gaze dropped to the medallion around Saegar's throat.

"I knew that you were one of the cursed ones," Locan said. "I wasn't sure where to look for you, on land or in the sea."

"And did you search?" Saegar asked, raising a brow.

Locan's mouth had a grim set as he nodded shortly. "Yes. I'm the one responsible for finding your two younger sisters, and I'm searching still for Thalassa. I need to find her. Badly. With her, Pacifica can be restored to its former greatness, and peace will reign over the kingdom once again."

Saegar's face softened at the sound of his sister's

name. "Aye," he said. "We need to find her, also. Only then will we know complete peace, especially now that I have learned my father has passed."

Beth thought about everything that had happened that day as she lay against her husband's shoulder in their bed that night. She thought of Kai and Phoebe and the happiness they'd found, of Thalassa, still lost to them all, and their father gone forever. But mostly she thought about Saegar, and Locan's remark.

"It doesn't seem fair, Saegar," she finally said softly.

Saegar rose on his elbow to look down at her face, lit by the moon shining gently in the window. "What does not, little one?"

"That your sisters, and even Locan, are mer and you're meremer. That they can change back and forth so easily, but you are cursed with legs now forever."

Saegar stroked his thumb over the sad droop of her mouth. Met the trouble in her eyes with a tender smile in his own.

Long, lonely years he'd wandered the seven seas waiting, he had thought, until he could return home to Pacifica. But now he knew what he'd really been waiting for—been searching for—was right here beside him.

Aye, he was overjoyed to be reunited with his sisters. But without Beth…without Beth he'd be lonely still. No matter where he was.

His arm tightened around her at the thought. He pulled her closer against his chest and bent to whisper in her ear, "Do you not know, my own, that every day I give thanks that you found me in the sea? That you kept me a captive until I emerged from the water to capture *you*?"

He kissed her hair, her temple, the silky skin of her cheek. He held her tighter still. "I am no longer cursed," he said, his voice husky from the emotion welling inside him. "Nay, I am forever blessed to have you."

Beth.

His mate. His wife. His love.

*   *   *   *   *

*Come back next month
for the thrilling conclusion to
the Silhouette Romance miniseries,*

A TALE OF THE SEA,

with Lilian Darcy's

FOR THE TAKING (RS #1620)

SILHOUETTE *Romance*™

**Lost siblings, secret worlds,
tender seduction—live the fantasy in...**

A TALE OF THE SEA

**Separated and hidden since childhood,
Phoebe, Kai, Saegar and Thalassa
must reunite in order to safeguard
their underwater kingdom.
But who will protect *them*...?**

*Look for these titles wherever
Silhouette books are sold!*

Silhouette®

Where love comes alive™

eHARLEQUIN.com

| | | community | membership |
| buy books | authors | online reads | magazine | learn to write |

Visit eHarlequin.com to discover your one-stop shop for romance:

buy books

♥ Choose from an extensive selection of Harlequin, Silhouette, MIRA and Steeple Hill books.

♥ Enjoy top Silhouette authors and *New York Times* bestselling authors in Other Romances: Nora Roberts, Jayne Ann Krentz, Danielle Steel and more!

♥ Check out our deal-of-the-week specially discounted books at up to 30% off!

♥ Save in our Bargain Outlet: hard-to-find books at great prices! Get 35% off your favorite books!

♥ Take advantage of our low-cost flat-rate shipping on all the books you want.

♥ Learn how to get FREE Internet-exclusive books.

♥ In our Authors area find the currently available titles of all the best writers.

♥ Get a sneak peek at the great reads for the next three months.

♥ Post your personal book recommendation online!

♥ Keep up with all your favorite miniseries.

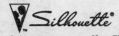

Silhouette®

where love comes alive™—online...

Visit us at
www.eHarlequin.com

SINTBB

SILHOUETTE *Romance*

COMING NEXT MONTH

#1618 THE WILL TO LOVE—Lindsay McKenna
Morgan's Mercenaries: Ultimate Rescue
With her community destroyed by an earthquake, Deputy Sheriff Kerry Chelton turned to Sergeant Quinn Grayson to help establish order and rebuild. But when Kerry was injured, Quinn began to realize that no devastation compared to losing Kerry....

#1619 THE RANCHER'S PROMISE—Jodi O'Donnell
Bridgewater Bachelors
Lara Dearborn's new boss was none other than Connor Brody—the son of her sworn enemy! Connor had worked his entire life to escape Mick Brody's legacy. But could he have a future with Lara when the truth about their fathers came out?

#1620 FOR THE TAKING—Lilian Darcy
A Tale of the Sea
Thalassa Morgan wanted to put the past behind her, something that Loucan—claimant of the Pacifica throne—wouldn't allow. Reluctantly she returned to Pacifica as his wife to restore order to their kingdom. But her sexy, uncompromising husband proved to be far more dangerous than the nightmares haunting her....

#1621 CROWNS AND A CRADLE—Valerie Parv
The Carramer Legacy
She thought she'd won a vacation to Carramer—but discovered her true identity! Sarah McInnes's grandfather was Prince Henry Valmont—and her one-year-old son the royal heir! Now, handsome, intense Prince Josquin had to persuade her to stay—but were his motives political or personal?

#1622 THE BILLIONAIRE'S BARGAIN—Myrna Mackenzie
The Wedding Auction
What does a confirmed bachelor stuck caring for his eighteen-month-old twin brothers do? Buy help from a woman auctioning her services for charity! But beautiful April Pruitt was no ordinary nanny, and Dylan Valentine wondered if his bachelorhood was the next item on the block!

#1623 THE SHERIFF'S 6-YEAR-OLD SECRET—Donna Clayton
The Thunder Clan
Nathan Thunder avoided intimate relationships—and discovering he had an independent six-year-old daughter wasn't going to change that! Gwen Fleming wanted to help her teenage brother. Could two mismatched families find true love?